Midsummer Adventures

Book 2 in The Guesthouse Girls Series

Judy Ann Koglin

Maui Shores Publishing

Kihei 2020

This book is a work of fiction. The characters within are fictitious. Any resemblance to any particular person is purely coincidental.

Summer Entanglements Copyright © 2020 by Maui Shores Publishing

Kihei, HI 96753
http://www.mauishorespublishing.com

Unless otherwise indicated, Scripture quotations are from: *The Holy Bible*, American Standard Version (ASV)

Library of Congress Control Number: 2020920953

ISBN 978-1-953799-02-9 (paperback)
ISBN 978-1-953799-03-6 (e-book)

CHAPTER ONE

Busy Week

The busy Fourth of July weekend was approaching, and fifteen-year-old Emma Martinez was excited to work extra hours as Femley's General Store prepared for extra-heavy crowds.

"I don't know how the crowds can get any heavier because the hotel rooms in Chelan are full every weekend during the summer," Emma commented to Mr. Femley, tossing her long curls behind her back so they wouldn't distract her.

"Oh, you'll see," Mr. Femley remarked. "Most of the local residents have out-of-town acquaintances who beg to let them stay with them or camp on their grass. People come and sleep in their truck beds and everywhere else you can imagine. People come from all over the state, Wenatchee, Seattle, Oregon, and Idaho. You'll see," he repeated.

Emma remembered from her job interview with Mr. Femley last spring that he looked forward to these big weekends like a little kid in a candy store. He planned his inventory carefully to try to ensure that he had exactly what he needed in stock to satisfy all the customers. It was evident to Emma that he had done a great job so far, and his business had stood the test of the time.

Emma, like many other high school and college students, had come to Chelan for the busy summer tourist season to help supplement the local workforce. Chelan was a three-hour drive from her home in Pasco.

She was especially fortunate because she was selected to stay at The Guesthouse, a summer boarding house just near the resort. Aunty Nola, as The Guesthouse proprietor Nola Milton liked to be called, accepted four girls each summer to stay at her place and work in town. Affordable accommodations were hard to come by during the summer season, so Aunty Nola opened up The Guesthouse at a reduced rate for summer workers, not only to give back to the town, but also because interacting with the girls helped keep her young. Aunty Nola chose the four girls from the 40 who had applied primarily based on their character and Nola's gut instinct about who needed to be there.

Emma was enjoying her summer immensely. She liked interacting with all the locals and the tourists who visited the general store where she worked. She also loved her roommates as if they were sisters. The girls who were extended invitations to stay at The Guesthouse along with Emma were Hope Stevens, a tall, athletic girl from Lynnwood; Kendi Arnold, an artistic and musical redhead from Redmond, and Amie Larson, a tiny, bubbly blonde girl who lived in Chelan but whose parents were out of state this summer taking care of Amie's grandpa, as he recovered from a back injury.

Emma had coordinated her Tuesday lunch break with Kendi's in order to discuss the upcoming Independence Day weekend. All of the Guesthouse Girls' parents were coming to town. It had been over a month since these parents had seen their daughters, and everyone was excited to be united with their families.

Promptly at noon, Emma and Kendi converged at the sandwich shop and stood in line to order their yummy sandwiches. Once they were handed the red baskets with their sandwiches, a pickle, and a chocolate-chip cookie, they proceeded to an outdoor table that was shaded by a bright blue umbrella.

3

Emma went over the plan of where everyone would be staying for the weekend: "So, my parents and Riley will stay in their timeshare; Amie will stay in her cousin's room near the resort since he's at camp; Hope's mom will stay in Amie's room at The Guesthouse; your parents have a room at the resort, and Amie's parents will be staying in a motor home on their property."

Kendi continued to outline their blueprint: "We'll all be busy working a lot, of course, but everyone said they could make it to the baptisms on Sunday and the late-night barbecue that we are doing at The Guesthouse on Saturday night. I'm glad we were all able to coordinate our schedules!"

"I'm so excited!" Emma said.

Kendi nodded in agreement. "It'll be a great weekend. I'll be so happy to see my parents and get baptized! What're you going to wear to the baptism?" she asked.

"I have a one-piece swimsuit that's black with little white triangles on it. I was thinking I'd wear that, but I don't know. I want something perfect. How about you?"

"I hadn't decided yet, but I have a one-piece that's light yellow. I don't wear it much because the color doesn't really look good on me. Does Femley's have a big selection of suits right now?"

"We're actually getting some more suits in today," Emma reported, her dark eyes sparkling. "I can't wait to see them! Come check them out after work and see if any of them would work for you."

The girls refilled their water bottles with cold filtered water from the glass container on the counter, then left their lunch table and headed back to work.

◊ ◊◊◊ ◊

At dinner Wednesday night, Aunty Nola told the girls that there might need to be a change in plans.

"Believe it or not, they just announced that we are expecting torrential rain this weekend," Aunty Nola said with a sigh. "The farmers will probably like it, but the vacationers will be really disappointed."

"Hopefully it won't be as bad as they're predicting?" Emma said optimistically.

"I'll keep an eye on the reports," Aunty Nola promised, "but I am also coming up with a Plan B for the barbecue."

◊ ◊◊◊ ◊

By Thursday, the weather was cooling down. Mr. Femley had changed the schedule because the store would be much slower since summer customers mostly shopped for beachwear, sunscreen, and towels. Demand would be curtailed if it rained.

"Emma, I hate to ask you this but, would you be okay with taking Saturday off if it rains?" Mr. Femley questioned.

"Not at all. I was originally excited to get some overtime hours, but I would be thrilled to be able to spend more time with my family!" she assured him.

◊ ◊◊◊ ◊

That evening, when Hope arrived at The Guesthouse after work, she shared similar news. "My uncle said that I will probably have Saturday off because, if we get rain, that will put the kibosh on most Jet Ski and party boat rentals."

Aunty Nola smiled. "Oh, that works out beautifully. When I first heard that rain was predicted, I booked the party room at the community center so we could move our late night barbecue indoors. Now that you and Emma are available earlier, we can have it at 5 o' clock!"

CHAPTER TWO

Fourth of July Weekend

Friday's weather actually started out promising. The morning sun shined down on the water and burned hot into the afternoon.

People who arrived in Chelan that morning were treated to a good day and some fun on the water. The girls were so excited to have their parents see them in action at their respective places of work.

Hope's mom came into town first, and she drove straight to her brother's watercraft rental shop where he had just finished his lunch.

Megan Stevens grinned at her brother. "Hi, Joe!"

Her brother Joe pulled her into a bear hug. "Hey, little sister! It's so good to finally see ya! What's it been, three years?" he asked.

"Not that long, but yes, *too* long." she admitted.

"I gotta tell you, Megan Stevens...you and your daughter look like twins, except for your height," Joe said. He also scrutinized her face. "You look really worn out. Meg, you need to take better care of yourself. You work too much."

"Thanks, Joe," Megan said sarcastically, before grinning. "I know that I probably have taken on too much this summer, but I wanted to take advantage of the time Hope is away to get in a lot of hours. I don't know how I am going to pull off college for her, but I need to try," she defended herself. "It's crazy to think that Hope is almost as old now as when I got pregnant with her. Where is my daughter, by the way?" she asked.

"She is over by the gas pump. She's heading this way now."

Hope caught a glimpse of her mother talking to Uncle Joe and she sprinted across the dock and enfolded her mama in a big bear hug.

"How was the drive, Mom? I missed you!" Hope sniffed a little bit in a rare show of emotion.

"I missed you too, honey," Megan said. "I am so excited for this weekend with you."

"How about if you ladies start the weekend now, Hope? Go ahead and get out of here." Joe pushed them gently toward Megan's car.

"Are you sure you don't need me?" Hope asked.

"Naw, get your mama settled in at The Guesthouse, and I'll meet you at Amigos for dinner at 7 o' clock." he insisted.

◊ ◊◊◊ ◊

Hope was excited to show her mom The Guesthouse and have her meet Aunty Nola in person. They had only met once this spring via Skype for Hope's interview to stay at the Guesthouse, so this was a special moment for them.

Aunty Nola embraced Megan with open arms just as Hope knew she would. Hope and Megan took the luggage to the room she would be using, and then they settled in on the couch to chat.

"Nola, I can't begin to thank you for taking in Hope this summer," Megan said, her tone a little quiet and shy. "She is so happy here, and she tells me about you all the time. She has never had an aunt or a grandma, so I think you fill that role for her."

Aunty Nola smiled at her compliments. "Thank you so much, my dear. I can tell where Hope gets her sweet spirit from. You share that quality. You also look so much alike."

Hope was secretly glad that the other girls were at work so that her mom could have uninterrupted time to sit down and get to know Aunty Nola.

9

Megan stayed downstairs talking with Aunty Nola and enjoyed a glass of iced tea and some treats from the tray Nola brought from the kitchen. Hope went upstairs and cleaned up from work, then joined her mom on the couch, cuddling up against her as the three of them talked.

Before long, Kendi came home with her parents in tow.

"Hi, Aunty Nola! I wanted to stop by a minute before we head out for dinner," Kendi said, evidently winded from the run up the entrance stairs. "Oh, you must be Hope's mom! I'm clearly stating the obvious. You look like sisters!" she said, her eyes wide.

They shook hands, and Megan gave an embarrassed "thank you."

"We get that a lot," Hope admitted.

Aunty Nola introduced the adults to each other, and they exchanged pleasantries while Kendi got dressed for dinner. She changed clothes quickly and returned downstairs to rejoin her parents.

"Bye, everyone! We'll probably be at the resort late tonight," Kendi told them.

"I would expect no less," Aunty Nola said affirmatively. "Enjoy this time as a family. We'll see you tomorrow," she said to Mr. and Mrs. Arnold. Kendi and her parents left for their car.

10

Emma and her family arrived a few minutes later, and a similar scene played out.

"Hi Nola," Emma's mom greeted her with a hug.

"Hi Nola!" Hank smiled with an upraised hand.

"It is so good to see you two. And Riley, you look taller than a month ago. Is that even possible?" Aunty Nola gushed.

Eleven-year-old Riley smile broadly. "I think I am taller!" she agreed.

"I'm going up to get my stuff. I'll be right back!" Emma announced.

Emma's eleven-year-old sister Riley had other ideas, and followed Emma upstairs when she went to get her stuff. "I want to see what you did to your room!" she explained.

While the girls were upstairs, Lina explained to Aunty Nola that they were going to get some pizza and then go swimming at their timeshare. When the girls came down, everyone exchanged goodbyes.

"We can't wait for tomorrow's barbecue," Hank winked at Nola.

"Mom, it's 6:40. We should think about going to meet Uncle Joe," Hope pointed out after Emma's family left.

"Oh, yes!" Aunty Nola exclaimed. "Sorry for keeping you so long. Would you like a ride?"

"I think we'll walk, Aunty Nola. Is that okay with you, Mom? I want to show you some things along the way."

"Fine with me," Megan said, game for anything.

◊ ◊◊◊ ◊

"So, Hope…how are you, really?" Hope's mom asked her once they left the house and walked a ways.

"Really good," Hope assured her. "There are some great running trails, and I've been able to stay in shape. The girls in The Guesthouse are like sisters, and Aunty Nola is…well, you've seen her. She's so nice!"

"And what about working for Uncle Joe?"

"He's amazing! He has always been kind of a dad to me. He's really funny and down to earth, and he's actually taught me a lot of tricks about how to manage a successful business. He's really smart," Hope reported.

"He always has been," Megan remembered. "Joe was seven years older than me, and he kind of took care of us after Mom and Dad died. He spent a lot of time with us in Lynnwood when you were a baby before he moved here full time. He will always have a special place in his heart for you, Hope."

12

As they were talking, Hope pointed to a street sign and the church just nearby. "Here is Cherry Street, and this is our church," she said proudly.

"I'm glad you are going to a church," Hope's mom said approvingly. "I never really went to church. Do you believe what they say?"

"I'm actually not sure yet. I've had some conversations with Aunty Nola. She's great and never pushy. She just answers my questions when she knows the answer and tells me to pray about it when it isn't specifically spelled out in the Bible."

"She is one cool lady." Hope's mom said admiringly. "I am a little jealous of you for getting to stay there."

"It's pretty great. We all love it here," Hope gushed, her eyes shining. "But I really miss you mom," Hope quickly added, hoping she hadn't hurt her mom's feelings.

"I know you do, pumpkin. I know that I don't give you the life you deserve, but thanks to Uncle Joe paying your rent at The Guesthouse, at least you are getting a wonderful summer."

Hope gave her mom a big hug, wishing on the inside that life wasn't so hard for her mom. She was the most selfless person that Hope had ever known, and she wished that someday she could be successful and help her mom to have a better life.

When they approached the restaurant past the church, Hope announced, "This is it!"

Uncle Joe was standing out front. "Right this way, ladies. I can taste the chips already!" he said, proudly opening the door for his sister and niece.

They settled into their booth and enjoyed Amigo's special enchilada plate while they caught up with each other's life updates.

As they were having after-dinner coffee, Joe asked, "Megan, would you like to meet me for an early breakfast tomorrow? We can go to the coffee shop near The Guesthouse. It is called Brandon's."

"Kendi works there," Hope told them both. "Remember meeting her at the house, Mom? She was the one with the red hair–not little Emma with the dark, curly hair."

"Yes, I remember Kendi," her mom laughed.

"So, Hope, could you go in early and work tomorrow while I'm at breakfast with your mom? We have two scheduled fishing boat rentals that will be there at about six in the morning. They are both regulars, and they come every summer. If the rain hits, I sincerely doubt we will get very many jet skiers unless they get so bored stuck in their hotel rooms that they decide to come anyway. Of course, it may not rain," he said with a doubtful look at the sky.

"Sure, I'll go in early," she replied tentatively, remembering an incident that happened earlier this summer when she was harassed by some guys who turned out to be car thieves. This is the first time she had ever been asked to work alone, so she was a little apprehensive.

Joe, remembering why Hope would be reluctant to work alone, assured her, "Ron will be in the shack with you. He won't be doing rentals. I have him doing a project organizing my files because I have to prepare some stuff for the bank, so you won't have to worry about being alone."

It gave Hope a sense of relief to know she would not be alone, but she was still a little disappointed not to go to breakfast with her mom and uncle. She was looking forward to having the weekend off. However, she wanted to work every bit she could to make extra cash, so she jumped at the chance.

The three of them stayed late at Amigos talking about old times when Megan was little and Uncle Joe was a teenager. Then they talked about how, when Joe played football and Megan sat on the bleachers with their parents cheering on the team.

"The guys on the team loved you! You were a little mascot for our team and sometimes, you even came to practice with me and sat really quietly."

"I recall," Megan smiled. "I knew every player!"

15

At one point, Uncle Joe looked up and noticed that they were the only ones still left in the restaurant. "It looks like they want to close down here," he said. "I'll take you ladies back to The Guesthouse, and you can hit the hay."

They drove home in tired silence, and when they arrived, Megan and Hope thanked Joe again for the dinner.

Uncle Joe gave Hope a few instructions for tomorrow morning and told Megan, "I'll pick you up at 6 o' clock. Love you both!"

As Hope finally went to sleep, she recalled that this was the happiest she had seen Uncle Joe. She never had heard him say the word "love" before, so she knew he must be in a good mood to see his little sister.

That makes two of us, Hope thought happily.

CHAPTER THREE

A Prosperous Saturday Morning

When her alarm dinged the next morning, Hope groaned as she heard the sound of rain pelting the room like a missile assault. She wondered if the people renting Uncle Joe's fishing boats would even show up.

She knew she needed to be there regardless, so she threw on her sweatshirt, pulled her hair through the opening in the back of a baseball cap, and jogged to the waterfront to start work.

Ron was already at work organizing paperwork, and Hope knew that Uncle Joe must have had him come early to give her peace of mind.

The weather did not seem to faze the first group of fishermen who were determined to enjoy their outing. Hope caught their enthusiasm.

17

"Thanks for showing up for us, young lady," a tanned older gentleman said to her as they were entering their boat. "Here is an extra something for you since I'm guessing you will have a pretty miserable shift in this weather," as he pushed a couple bills in her hand.

Hope thanked him for the tip but didn't have a chance to look at it because she was in a hurry to get back to the rental shack for shelter. She shoved the wet money into the pocket of her frayed denim shorts as she saw the next pair of customers approaching.

"You look like you have been in the rain for hours already," the thin man dressed in green outdoorsman-looking clothing commented cheerfully.

"Are you still planning on fishing?" Hope asked skeptically, looking toward the sky.

"Oh yeah, we are!" his pudgier companion said enthusiastically. "I have the best luck on rainy days."

Hope got them outfitted with lifejackets and checked the boat out to them. They were friendly and jovial as they handed her a $20 bill for a tip. *Wow! Two in a row!* Hope thought enthusiastically. *Uncle Joe has been holding out on me. Jet skiers rarely tip. Maybe I can do more of these early shifts.*

She closed the door of the shack behind her and pulled the other tip from her pocket. She was surprised to see that the two bills were fifty dollars each. *$120 in less than a half hour! That was the best half hour I'll probably ever have,* Hope thought as she laughed.

The day passed uneventfully. After straightening up the paperwork, Hope spent time on her phone watching a video about the best stretches to do to prevent different kinds of injuries.

Joe called at one point and said that he gave the other two employees a day off since there were very few watercraft renters likely to go out. He mentioned that he and Hope's mom were going to take care of a few things, and he would come and take over around a little later if she could hold down the fort.

Hope assured him that she could and hung up, feeling good that he could trust her with his business. She had a fleeting thought wondering what he and her mom needed to do, but she dismissed it and went back to watching her video.

By about ten o' clock, the rain had subsided, but it was still dreary. A few brave people straggled in for their Jet Ski rides, not bothered a bit by the rain. An hour later, a family arrived, and Hope got them set up and sent them off buzzing across the lake.

Upon their return an hour later, the dad said they had a great time and handed Hope a twenty-dollar bill.

Just before noon, three more people came: a grandma, her middle-aged daughter, and a granddaughter who looked to be about 19 years old. Hope got them situated for their Jet Ski ride and laughed at the spunky grandma's zest for life. *This is what Emma will be like when she's old,* Hope mused with a chuckle.

Right after that, Joe arrived with Hope's mom. They both seemed very upbeat.

"Kendi's mom is taking the other girls shopping in Wenatchee and wanted to know if we wanted to go, too," Megan explained. "I told her I would check with you. I thought it sounded fun. They are leaving at 12:30, so we need to get back to The Guesthouse so you can change, and we can go if you want."

"Sure! That sounds great if you want to," Hope said tentatively, gripping the $140 in tips she had made today. She knew that she wanted to buy something special for her mom with some of the money, and this would be a perfect opportunity. "We'd better run to catch them before they leave," she said while glancing at the clock displayed on her phone.

20

The two of them jogged back to The Guesthouse and managed to miss most of the rain that started up again when they were almost home. When they got back, they were greeted by a crowd of ladies.

Hope went upstairs to change and dry her hair. When she returned, her mother commented, "Your hair looks amazing. I've never seen you blow it out like that, and I can't believe how blond it got already this summer!"

"I know," Hope grinned. "Probably because I'm outside in the sun 24/7!"

Are you sure you want to go, Hope? I know you don't love to shop."

"No, I want to go, Mom. I want you to get to know the girls. They're the best!" Hope surprised even herself with her enthusiasm.

"Sounds good! I think everyone is ready to load up." Hope's mom said with a smile.

Judy Ann Koglin

CHAPTER FOUR

Sales and Surprises

"Nola thanks so much for letting us use your van," Kendi's mom said from the driver's seat. Next to her, Emma's mom nodded in agreement.

In the second row, Emma, her little sister Riley, and Kendi chatted and giggled. In the back seat, Amie, Hope, and Hope's mom Megan got to know each other.

"You look like you could be one of The Guesthouse Girls," Amie spoke conspiratorially to Hope's mom.

"Well, I had Hope when I was only 16, so I am younger than the average mom, but I definitely don't look like a teenager," Megan responded with a laugh. "Plus, you are as young as you feel, and I feel about 65," she added wryly.

This started a lively conversation between Amie and Hope's mom. Megan asked Amie a bunch of questions about her high school, the athletics at her school, her friends, and Chelan in general. Amie answered all her questions knowledgably, and Hope thought to herself that Amie could be a really good tour guide some day. Amie even looked the part with her cute blond bob and impeccable style.

With all the chatter in the van, the hour-long ride went by fast. Pretty soon, they arrived at Wenatchee Mall.

"We have about two hours here," Kendi's mom announced. "Let's split up, but everyone has to have at least one other person with them at all times…except the moms, of course. We'll meet at the cosmetics counter by the entrance of Macy's at exactly 4 o' clock. Do not leave the mall or go to the parking lot without checking with an adult. Sound okay to everybody?"

Everyone agreed, and the girls split up; Emma and her mom Lina and sister Riley were one group and went off towards Claire's to look at accessories.

Kendi and her mom Beth, along with Amie, set their sights on Macy's. "I want to see the new fall collections," Amie said to Kendi as they headed in that direction.

Megan asked Hope what she wanted to do. "I think we could just walk around and talk. Maybe we could go to Jamba Juice and get something to drink," Hope said. "I got some tip money today, so it's my treat," she added proudly.

"That sounds great. I have some things to talk to you about."

"What, Mom?" Hope asked with a frown. All kinds of things went through her mind, none of them good.

"Nothing bad, honey…at least I don't *think* it will be bad," Megan began.

When they had reached Jamba Juice, Hope ordered a peanut butter and banana smoothie, and Megan ordered blackberry lemonade. Hope proudly paid for both.

"Thanks, honey, that is very sweet of you, but I am doing fine. I have been working a lot since you have been gone. I am ahead on the bills and have extra saved for sports fees."

"Wow, that's great, mom!" Hope replied. "What did you want to talk to me about?" she asked nervously.

"Well, it all started this morning at breakfast with Joe. He told me that he had an opportunity to totally expand his business by purchasing the sporting goods store across from where you work.

25

If he bought the store, it would enable him to combine his current summer business with the snowboard and ski rentals that the sporting goods store normally does during the winter. He would also be able to sell golf and fishing gear, balls, and other sports equipment."

"Wow, that's fantastic!" Hope said enthusiastically. "I wonder why he didn't tell me."

"Well, it's not a done deal yet, so he probably didn't want to jinx it. But there is more to the story…a lot more," Megan went on. "I didn't know this, but the whole time he's been living here, Joe has been renting his room in the cute little house on Maple Street.
It was actually a rent-to-own situation, and he has made his last payment last year and now owns the whole house. The lady who owned it, Edith, is going to move in with her daughter down in Florida later this fall, and Joe will have the house to himself."

"That's awesome!" Hope said, "Good for him!"

"Here is the rest of the story," her mother continued, "Joe wanted to know if we would want move in with him when the other lady moves away. I could work for him full-time at the hardware store, and you could go to school in Chelan and do sports there."

Hope sat in stunned silence for a minute and then was surprised to find that she had tears in her eyes.

Seeing that, Megan quickly backpedaled. "I'm so sorry honey! We totally don't have to do this. It was just an idea Uncle Joe had. Don't worry; I promise I won't drag you away from your school, your friends, and your teams in the middle of high school!" Now her mom had tears, too.

"No, mom!" Hope cried, giving her mom a hug. "I *want* to move to Chelan. It's like a dream come true!" she exclaimed breathlessly.

"Oh, I'm so glad," Megan said. "I think it will be a much better life for both of us. Our apartment back home is in such a bad part of town. I want you to feel safe, and I can tell how happy you seem here. Plus, being with Uncle Joe would be good."

"Well, I'm in." Hope then got practical. "What's the next step?"

"Well, I asked Joe about that at breakfast. He suggested that I go home and keep working at my jobs…at least one of them, for now. Remember, we still don't know if this deal will go through, but it's looking good right now. However, assuming that it works out, a couple weeks before the lady he lives with moves to Florida, I'll give my notice at work, and then we can move into Uncle Joe's house."

"Hmmm…what if that's mid-season?" Hope speculated.

"Actually, it will probably be around November, so it will be in the middle of soccer. So, Joe and I had a talk with Aunty Nola after breakfast, and she said not to worry. She had some ideas we could discuss with her later."

"So, is it all settled? Are we going to do this?" Hope asked expectantly.

"Let's say that there is a strong possibility, but each of us will have to work through some details to make it happen…particularly Uncle Joe" her mom said. "Let's hold off on telling others until it is a sure thing."

"Sounds good, Mom, but I don't think I'll be able to wipe the smile off my face."

"Me neither," her mom replied with a grin. "Let's go check out the new scents at Bath and Body Works," she suggested.

"That works for me, Mom!" Hope said, taking her mom's arm. The two practically skipped down the mall together, more joyful than they had been in a long time.

◊ ◊◊◊ ◊

Promptly at four o' clock, the group met up at their designated meeting place inside Macy's and excitedly reported on their shopping successes.

Emma had purchased some dangly earrings at Claire's that were marked down 70%, along with a super-cute scoop-neck pink t-shirt and white shorts from Macy's that were on a summer clearance sale. Amie bought a couple shopping bags full of new fall fashions and shoes. Kendi purchased a bag from one of the smaller stores that contained a cute blue and white striped summer dress, a violet one-piece swimsuit, and a small bag with a couple items from the sale at Claire's. In her other hand, she carried a small shopping bag from Bath and Body Works. Hope had a bag with some tan capris, a nice pair of shorts, and even a cute lime green dress she had found on clearance. She also found a pink romper for her mom that she had insisted on buying with part of her tip money. Kendi and Emma's moms both had shopping bags in their hands as well.

"Okay, ladies, it is hard to be the bad guy, but I think we need to get on the road if we are going to make it back in time for dinner," Kendi's mom Beth announced.

Everyone gathered up their colorful shopping bags and started walking toward the exit closest to their van.

However, on their way to the door, Kendi spied a big shoe rack that said 50% off clearance sandals.

Amie and Kendi scampered over and quickly scanned the racks. There were shoes with high heels, some that were slightly elevated, and even some sparkly flip flops.

"These are only six dollars after all the discounts," Kendi yelped, beckoning the rest of the moms and daughters to join the two of them.

Each of the girls found a couple pairs that would fit them and even the moms and Riley got in on the good deals and bought some of the newly-marked-down sandals.

"You were in the right place at the right time," the sales lady said merrily as she watched how thrilled they were with their great finds. "I'd love to take a group photo of you with your purchases for our store newsletter. Would that be okay?"

Everyone agreed, and they displayed their Macy's bags prominently for the photo. The lady also snapped a photo with the girls' cameras and asked that they share it on social media to get the word out about the sales.

"Sure thing!" Amie replied gamely, and she posted immediately, tagging the others.

"Now we *really* have to go!" Lina said, looking at her phone. The eight happy ladies, both young and older, piled into the van, their happy chatter filling the air for the next hour until they arrived home.

◊ ◊◊◊ ◊

As they were pulling into the rainy Chelan Community Center parking lot, Emma mentioned that they already received 100 likes and 30 comments on their photo. "Look! We got likes from Ryan and Ben already!" she squealed.

Ryan Sanders and Ben Brandon were two good-looking local boys who were part of their friend group here in Chelan. Both boys were tall; Ryan looked like a teenage version of Zac Efron with his brown hair and brown eyes, and Ben had bushy blond surfer hair and blue eyes.

They walked into the community center and saw that their families had assembled in the large room that bordered the lake. Aunty Nola and Amie's mom Staci were setting up barbecued chicken and ribs as well as an assortment of salads that were brought over from Stillwaters, the resort's restaurant. The dads were setting up the dining chairs, and Uncle Joe was wiping down the tables.

Hope went over to her uncle and gave him a big wordless hug. Uncle Joe deduced from Hope's rare display of affection that her mom had given her the lowdown on the potential move, and Hope must have been on board with the possibility. He smiled.

The four families and Aunty Nola sat down together for a delicious feast.

Aunty Nola stood in front of them for a little opening speech. "I want thanking everyone for sharing your daughters with me this summer. I've never had children of my own so I really enjoy being Aunty Nola to your wonderful young ladies."

The group smiled and Emma's dad yelled, "No, thank *you*! Anyone willing to take on four teenage girls is a *saint*!" That comment brought out chuckles and nods from the parents and giggles from the girls.

Nola smiled and then asked them all to bow so she could thank God for the delicious-smelling food. Then, after she had blessed the food and everyone had filled their plates, Aunty Nola stood up again.

"I had a little activity that I thought would be fun to do during dinner. I would like each of the girls to share the favorite thing they have done so far this summer, along with one thing they are looking forward to.

Emma volunteered to go first. "Um, my favorite thing was the Slip and Slide water park party that we went to a few weeks ago. We went on all the slides, and the lazy river, and I became a Christian that night."

"That was a special night," Nola confirmed.

"And what are you looking forward to?" Aunty Nola prompted.

"Lots of things," Emma squealed. "Starting with tomorrow when I get baptized!"

"What's 'get baptized?'" Riley asked.

Emma tried to come up with an explanation that her sister would easily understand: "Baptism is when you become a Christian and you want other people to know about it, so the pastor dunks you underwater."

Riley gave her older sister a confused look.

"Think of it this way, Riley," Amie offered, "when someone asks Jesus to come into their life and forgive their sins, it can be done quietly, just by praying, and other people don't always know about it. When you get baptized, it symbolizes becoming a new person. Going down in the water symbolizes that your old self died, and coming up from the water shows that you're alive, but this time, you have Jesus inside you. You get baptized publicly to show everyone that you are proud to be a Christian and don't want to hide it."

"Oh," Riley said, still looking a bit puzzled.

"We'll talk about it more later tonight," Emma assured her. "Let's give Kendi a chance to answer the questions. I'm curious what was her favorite part of the summer so far."

Kendi began, "Well, my favorite thing so far was being able to work during the concerts at the coffee shop and getting to sing during karaoke events there. "The thing I'm looking forward to the most is the same as Emma: getting baptized tomorrow."

When it was Amie's turn, she stood up and announced, "I really enjoyed the beach party the first night that the other girls arrived, and I also love working at the front desk of Lakeshore Resort, where my family works. My job is about to change a little bit and I am looking forward to being trained in other areas at the resort starting Monday because I want to learn about the whole place."

When it was Hope's turn, she wasn't sure what to say, especially because she now had a huge secret to keep about the fact that they might be moving here. She decided to keep it simple. "I love that I get to spend time with my Uncle Joe, work outdoors, and have three new best friends," she said, smiling at The Guesthouse Girls, "but my very favorite thing has been my morning talks with Aunty Nola," she added, sending Nola a fond look.

"Oh, thank you, dear," Aunty Nola said with emotion. "And what are you looking forward to?"

"Just more of the same," Hope said with a hidden meaning she hoped Aunty Nola and her mom and uncle would catch.

The girls cleaned up the disposable plates and utensils and gathered up the paper tablecloths and threw them away. The moms and Aunty Nola packaged up the leftover food to be sent back to The Guesthouse. The men folded up the tables and chairs and returned them to the closet as per the instructions they received from the manager of the community center.

While all of this was in progress, Kendi's phone beeped to signal a text from Ryan. He wanted to know if they would like to hang out with them at the arcade at his parent's water park.

"Slip and Slide is closed," the text read, "but we can use the side door and play games in the arcade for an hour or so if you want. Tell all the parents they can come, too, if they're bored."

The rain was still coming down, and the girls decided that the arcade would be a fun diversion.

Emma's parents and Riley decided to come, too, as did Hope's mom. Kendi's parents went for a drive around the lake. Aunty Nola had some things to do and joked about not really being an arcade-type person. Amie's mom and dad headed back to the office at the resort because they had lots to do there while they were in town. Joe went back to look over the paperwork that Ron had organized for him earlier in the day.

All thanked Aunty Nola for organizing the event and thanked Amie's parents for supplying the delicious food that they insisted on providing free of charge.

◊ ◊◊◊ ◊

Everyone dispersed, and the four girls and Riley headed to the arcade with Mr. and Mrs. Martinez and Ms. Stevens. When they got there, Ryan gave them each a cup of tokens, and they went around playing games.

Kendi and Hope wandered over to the more athletic games on the side wall where they found Ryan and Ben. The boys challenged Hope to a free throw competition where they each manned one of the three side-by-side basketball shot games. Hope had sunk four shots before either of the boys had gotten two shots.

Kendi was cheering for Hope, and soon, Amie and Emma had come over and had joined with cheers of "Go Hope! Girl Power! Win one for the Guesthouse Girls!"

The boys laughingly protested that Hope had an unfair advantage due to her cheering section, as they shot their basketballs. The competition grew even more intense when Ryan rallied and caught up to Hope when they both reached twelve shots.

Not to be outdone, Ben put on the gas. So far, the scores were as follows: Ben 15, Hope 14, and Ryan 13. By then, parents had come over and had joined in the excitement. When the time elapsed, Hope finished up with a whopping 18, while Ryan got 17, and Ben was still at 15. Inspired, Emma's parents and Hope's mom decided to give it a go.

Later, everyone dispersed and shuffled around as they saw fit. The four girls wandered over to the four-person air hockey table, and Amie and Hope challenged Kendi and Emma to a game. The girls played an enthusiastic round with Hope and Amie emerging with the victory.

Emma's mom and dad played multiple games of Ms. Pac Man. Then, Ben and Ryan's friend Cody, a lanky boy with brown hair showed up, and he and Amie played Whack-a-Mole with Hope and her mom. Ryan and Ben challenged Kendi and Emma to an air hockey game, which the boys won handily. Ryan, Ben, and Cody headed over to play a shooting game, and everyone else gravitated to games they liked.

Emma's mom had lost track of where Riley was but soon found her in front of a pink Hello Kitty game where she had been for the whole time, racking up lots and lots of points. Ryan promised that she could redeem the tickets on their next visit.

After a while, Ryan regretfully broke the news that he needed to close the arcade down in about 15 minutes. Everyone finished their last couple games and thanked Ryan profusely for opening up the arcade for them.

"We'll see you tomorrow at church," Emma called to the boys as they drove off.

CHAPTER FIVE

Independence Day

The Fourth of July ended up having a lot better weather than the day before. Kendi and Emma had swimsuits under their dresses so they could be ready for the baptisms in the lake.

After church, the whole congregation walked two blocks to the park where the church had an area reserved. Emma and Kendi gathered in a huddle with the pastor, the youth pastor, and six other people who were going to be baptized that day. The head pastor explained that he was going to baptize the adults, and the youth pastor would baptize the four teens and pre-teens. The two pastors had the eight people who were getting baptized stand in a row, facing the bright sunshine and the crowd of church members and visitors.

Kendi and Emma were the last ones in the line. "This may look like a firing squad but it isn't, so put your weapons away," he quipped to the onlookers.

He went down the row and asked each participant if they had accepted Christ as their Savior and why they wanted to be baptized.

When it was Kendi's turn she looked at the crowd and stated, "My name is Kendi and I accepted Christ as my Savior a few weeks ago and I am getting baptized today as an outward expression of an inward change."

Emma went next. *Why do I always have to follow Kendi? She is always so eloquent!* She cleared her throat and began, "Hi, I'm Emma. I became a Christian recently and I am getting baptized today to show people that I really want to live a life that pleases Him."

This concluded the short testimonies and the two pastors led the group down to the water's edge. Each person went out when it was their turn. When Kendi's name was called, she self-consciously waded out until she was waist-deep in the water and arrived at the area with the youth pastor. His voice boomed, "Kendi Arnold, based on your confession of faith, I baptize you in the name of the Father, the Son, and the Holy Spirit."

He then put one hand behind her head, and one hand on her stomach and carefully leaned her back and briefly submerged her, then pulled her right back up. Kendi raised her hands in a sort of victorious pose and the whole crowd clapped and celebrated.

Then, it was Emma's turn and she followed the same process that Kendi just experienced. She was so short that the water came up almost to her shoulders. The youth pastor had her take a couple steps toward the shore so she would be waist deep. After the pastor dunked her and pulled her out of the water, she also raised her hands up and then quickly made her way to shore where her mom had a fluffy yellow towel waiting to wrap her up in.

Afterwards, Aunty Nola and Amie presented both Kendi and Emma with flowers and parents hugged their wet daughters. It was a special moment filled with selfies and laughter.

But very soon after the baptism was over, their group regretfully had to disband because of various obligations. Amie's parents needed to go back to the resort to do some paperwork while they were in town, Hope and Emma needed to get back to their respective places of work since the unexpected sunny day required all hands on deck.

Emma's parents and Riley headed back to their timeshare to go swimming, and Kendi's parents went to the coffee shop to see their daughter in action and to meet the Brandons, her employers.

◊ ◊◊◊ ◊

Hope's mom Megan headed back to The Guesthouse with Nola.

They sat down at the table and had a huge heart-to-heart talk. Megan was surprised how easy it was to talk to Aunty Nola, and it was evident that she was a very kind and wise woman, just as Hope had said. Megan found herself opening up to Nola and telling her things she had never told anyone, not even Hope. Megan was met with nothing but compassion and love from Nola, and the conversation progressed throughout the afternoon.

Aunty Nola asked Megan when she thought she would be able to move to Chelan.

"I think around mid-November." Megan began. "The landlord at my brother's house, Edith, wants to get moved before the snow begins...*former* landlord," she corrected herself.

"Excellent, my dear. My idea should work out perfectly."

"What idea?" Megan asked, smiling.

"Well, I wanted to see if you thought Hope would be willing to stay here up until your move.

She could go to school at Chelan High and play soccer there, and she can keep me company. Then, when you are ready, and Edith moves to Florida, both of you can move into Joe's house. It would really be a treat to me to have Hope around before I start renting the place to skiers and winter retreat groups. That usually doesn't begin until late November."

"Oh, Aunty Nola, that would so cool! But Joe paid for her to be here this summer, and I don't know if he will want to keep doing it since he will be buying the new business."

"Oh no, honey, this would be my treat, and, selfishly, it would be really nice for me not to be alone in this big house all autumn. Hope would be right here to have a front row seat to the apple harvest, and there will be plenty of room for you to stay here on weekends any chance you get." Nola went on enthusiastically.

"I think Hope would love that arrangement." Megan agreed. "I can't wait to see her face when you ask her!"

"Let's talk to her tonight if we get a chance and no one else is around. Megan, you look exhausted. This has been a lot for you! How about if we both go and try to get some rest before everyone else gets here. It will probably be a late night."

"A nap sounds wonderful," Megan agreed, and they each slept peacefully for the next two hours.

◊ ◊◊◊ ◊

At around half past five, Kendi came home from work, changed quickly, and headed over to the resort to meet her parents for dinner.

A little later, Emma stopped by The Guesthouse briefly with her parents to grab a few things, and her parents whisked her off so she could spend some time with them at their timeshare and watch the fireworks from there.

After a while, Hope arrived, and she, her mom, and Aunty Nola ate a late dinner of leftover ribs and chicken from the night before.

Over dinner, Aunty Nola presented her plan to have Hope stay until mid-November and Hope happily agreed.

"That means I can play soccer here if everything works out!" Hope exclaimed.

Aunty Nola asked Megan and Hope if they would prefer to watch fireworks from the front porch, or if they would like to watch them from the beach park. They decided to walk to the beach park where they would have a closer view to the barge that was setting off the display.

It was dusk when they arrived, and they were lucky enough to get the last remaining picnic table.

They settled in with blankets to see the festivities.

It wasn't long before a group of teenagers walked by.

"Oh, hi, Hope!" one of the boys said upon seeing her. It was Brett, one of the local boys she met on her first weekend in town. He came over to talk.

Upon hearing Hope's name, Conner broke away from the group and jogged over to the picnic table. Hope introduced her mom and Aunty Nola to the two boys.

"Oh, I've known Conner for years," Aunty Nola shared. "I am friends with his grandma."

Conner grinned in response.

They were interrupted by the announcer's voice welcoming them to the annual Fourth of July show. Conner asked if they could join the ladies at the picnic table, and Aunty Nola cheerfully agreed.

The five of them enjoyed the elaborate show immensely. The town had spared no expense to have a fantastic celebration, and the weather cooperated beautifully. Hope was mesmerized by the colorful explosions of light: first purple, then yellow, then green, then silver. When those finished, there was another explosion with red, white, and blue, and they just continued to pop and whistle, bringing beautiful explosions of color, each more spectacular than the last.

Finally, Conner enthusiastically alerted the table that he thought the next one was the grand finale. He was right. It was long, loud, colorful, and magical, all at the same time.

Afterwards, all five at the picnic table declared this to be the best fireworks show they'd ever seen.

Before long, Hope told the boys that she, her mom, and Aunty Nola were leaving.

The boys said polite goodbyes to the ladies as they were folding up their blankets, and Conner touched Hope's arm to get her attention. "Hey, Hope, I'm glad we ran into you tonight. Maybe I'll rent a jet ski sometime," he said with a wink.

"I don't know, they're pretty expensive," Hope replied with a twinkle in her eye.

"It'll be worth it," Conner assured her and went off to meet up with his friends.

The three ladies walked home, and Hope reflected on what an amazing weekend she had with the Saturday morning unexpected tip money, a fun shopping trip, the great news about possibly staying here full-time, the baptisms, the fireworks, and the short talk with Conner at the end of the night.

As Hope nestled her head on her pillow and pulled her comforter around her, she fell asleep feeling happier than she ever had before.

CHAPTER SIX

House Hunting

After years of thinking about it, Kendi and her parents decided to look for an investment property in Chelan. The plan was to rent it to vacationers most of the time in the summer but be able to block it off to use themselves whenever they wanted to.

Kendi accompanied her parents on their house hunting whenever she wasn't working over the course of the week. The artist in her loved to look at the different architecture and décor ideas, and it was interesting to see how the homes were designed to maximize the views and the space.

Most of the condos and houses that they wanted to see were occupied with renters, so they couldn't walk inside, but they were able to walk on some of their grounds and get an idea of the neighborhood.

47

The realtor supplied interior photos for them to view as well.

Kendi would come to work each afternoon with stories about the places they toured.

"I've never gone house hunting before. This seems just like the show on TV that my mom loves to watch," Ben exclaimed.

"It is so much fun," Kendi admitted. "My family does this kind of thing a lot. I think my mom should be a realtor."

After seeing how much fun Kendi was having, Ben was intrigued. "I would love to check out the places," Ben mentioned.

"Why don't you come with us tomorrow?" Kendi suggested.

"Do you think your parents would mind?" Ben questioned.

"No, they would love for you to come!"

So, on Thursday, the real estate agent drove with Kendi's parents in her Mercedes Benz, and Ben and Kendi followed in his little gray car. They walked the grounds of Manawa Valley, a new upscale condominium complex, a few miles out of town.

The realtor told them proudly that this property had a model home that they could walk through. Kendi's parents were awed by the views and the luxurious furnishings in the spacious model home.

Kendi and Ben really loved the amenities. There was a fully equipped gym, an indoor and three outdoor pools, a party room with dance floor that could be reserved for wedding receptions, an outdoor lakeside area designed with a gazebo for special occasions, and numerous other special features.

"Maybe we'll get married here," Ben whispered while the adults were occupied with house touring. Kendi laughed at his comment. "Oh, really? Who are you marrying?"

"Probably some poor girl who runs out of other options," he joked with a smirk. "How about you?"

"Maybe I'll remain single and be a career bridesmaid," Kendi responded.

"So...couples can rent a venue complete with an extra bridesmaid, if needed?"

Kendi nodded. "Yeah, something like that. They'll have to buy me the dress each time, though."

"My wife and I will keep that in mind if we need an extra bridesmaid," Ben quipped. The two of them laughed at their silliness as they joined her parents and the realtor.

Kendi's parents really loved the condo, but the price tag was staggering, even for them. Kendi's mom commented, "It's a bit out of our budget."

"What some people do is go in with another couple and run it like a business. Then, they divide both the expenses and the income," the realtor suggested optimistically.

"Hmmm… that would be an interesting proposition," Mr. Arnold mused, but his wife shook her head.

"I think we should stick with places where we don't need a partner," Kendi's mom stated. The realtor pulled out some more papers and told them they had several more places to see.

Ben and Kendi followed them around to three more potential properties. During the drive to the last property, Ben mentioned to Kendi that he was starving.

"Maybe after this one, my parents can jump into your car and we can go to lunch?" Kendi suggested.

"That sounds great," Ben replied, rubbing his flat stomach.

When they arrived at the last house, Kendi pulled her dad aside and made arrangements.

She told Ben it was all settled. After viewing this house and deciding the price was right, but the location was too far from the lake, Kendi's parents buckled into the back seat of Ben's car and suggested that they head to Beaches, at the resort.

Kendi felt a little weird sitting in the front seat with a boy with her parents in the backseat. That made her mind wander about how it would feel if Ben was her boyfriend instead of just a friend and coworker. He was tall and blond with a great tan and mesmerizing smile. He was confident, but not arrogant. He shared her love of music and espresso. He was a strong Christian and would probably be a good boyfriend to someone. Kendi wondered why he didn't already have a girlfriend. Maybe he had a recent break-up. She decided that she might want to ask Amie about that sometime. She knew Emma would be thrilled to date him.

◊ ◊◊◊ ◊

Ben parked the car at the resort, and the sound of the car stopping snapped her out of her musings. The lunch crowd was waning, and the four of them found a table and sat down. They were greeted by their waiter Josh, a friend who had just graduated from Chelan High. Ben introduced Josh to Kendi's parents, and Kendi asked if Amie was working.

Josh's face lit up at the mention of her name. "She's actually in the back. I'll let her know you're here," Josh said, grinning as he handed out menus.

"What's good here?" Kendi's parents asked Ben.

"I'm more of a quantity eater, so I'm not too picky about what I eat," Ben admitted.

"That reminds me of how I was at your age. I ate everything I could get my hands on." Kendi's dad laughed, remembering. "Just a warning: you may not be able to do that forever."

"That's what my dad tells me and my brother. He used to be able to eat like a horse and not gain weight, but somewhere along the way he had to stop and watch his beer gut. Well, he actually doesn't drink beer, only wine sometimes..." Ben trailed off in embarrassment.

"Exactly," Mr. Arnold agreed. "Us older guys need moderation if we want impress our women."

Kendi felt like the conversation was getting weird, so she changed the subject: "I think I'll have a half BLT with a side salad."

"Oh, that sounds good," her mom agreed.

Kendi's dad and Ben both ordered today's special, which was a crab melt on sourdough with a cup of tomato soup.

After they placed their orders, Amie emerged from the kitchen and came by to greet them.

"Welcome to Beaches," she smiled warmly. "Did you order the special?"

"My dad and Ben did," Kendi confirmed. My mom and I ordered the BLT and a side salad."

"Also a great choice," Amie assured her. "What have you all been up to today?" Amie asked.

They described their house-hunting adventure and chatted for a few minutes then Amie excused herself to go back to her duties and thanked them for coming in.

When she left, Kendi's mom commented, "She carries herself like she is the manager."

"I know," Kendi said with a smile. "Amie is just like that. She exudes friendliness and confidence."

"Well, it looks like our waiter likes her," noted Kendi's mom.

"Yeah, I think it might be mutual," Kendi murmured. She then changed the subject quickly: "Which house was your favorite?" This turned into a lively discussion that was reminiscent of the decision scenes from House Hunters on TV. This conversation lasted all the way until the last bite was eaten.

On the way out, Mr. Arnold remarked that their perfect house had not found them yet.

"I agree. I think we'll know it when we see it. Maybe we can look again in the fall when the renters go home and we can actually tour the inside of places," Mrs. Arnold suggested.

"Good idea, hon. Maybe October would be good," Mr. Arnold agreed.

Kendi's dad asked her if she wanted to come by later to swim and she said "yes" enthusiastically.

Her parents went to their room, and Ben drove Kendi back to The Guesthouse.

"I like your parents," Ben mentioned on the drive.

"Yeah! I got lucky in that department, just like you did," Kendi responded. "Well, thanks for coming with us and for driving," she said, jumping out of the car and waving goodbye.

"My pleasure!" he called out the window as he drove away smiling.

CHAPTER SEVEN

Veggies and Ducks

When Ben, Kendi, and her parents were leaving the Beaches lunch counter, Amie was busy back in the kitchen, prepping food for dinner service for the resort's more formal restaurant, Stillwaters.

She was shaving radishes and carrots with an instrument that looked like a small vegetable peeler. When she did it properly, they would come out curled, and then Amie would add them to a bowl of water so they could stay looking perfect for when the cooks used them as a garnish.

When she had filled the bowl, she asked the prep cook for her next task. He had her refill all the spice containers so they would be ready for the cooks to use. It was a menial task, but it was needed, and it required little supervision.

Amie's next task was to cut red, yellow and green peppers in neat little slices to be used in fajitas and salads. Then, she prepped several batches of the resort's ever-popular strawberry lemonade.

After all the prep, at long last, her shift was over for the day. Josh was getting off work at the same time and they exited the resort together.

"Hey Amie!" Josh greeted her. "How did you like working dinner prep today?"

"To be honest, it wasn't my favorite."

Josh gave her a sympathetic nod. "I agree; I much prefer working with customers than cutting vegetables in the kitchen. But lucky for us, there are a lot of people who would rather work in the kitchen and let us deal with the customers."

"Hopefully, I'll be able to start training on the front-of-house stuff soon," Amie said wistfully.

"I'm sure you will. I think they're going to have you do more bussing and possibly some serving during the rest of the month."

Amie brightened. "Oh that'll be so much better!"

"Hey, I was thinking of heading over to the park to watch the boats for a while. You wanna come?"

Amie nodded and put up her finger toward him in a gesture to wait just a minute while she responded to a long text that her parents had sent.

After she was done with her phone, she looked up and answered, "Sure, I can come for a while. My parents are going to work for another hour, and then we're going to grab something to eat at Amigos."

"Are you having fun at The Guesthouse?" Josh asked as they walked.

"Yes, I love the girls. Sometimes, we end up staying up way too late just laughing. We're like sisters who don't fight with each other."

"That's so cool."

"Yeah, and Aunty Nola is incredible. She has certain nights that she schedules us all to be home so we can talk to each other and share what's going on in our lives so we can help each other."

"Boy troubles?" Josh teased.

Amie laughed. "Maybe, but our talks tend to be more like life troubles. Sometimes, they're about someone's work or someone's family, or maybe something spiritual. Each talk we have is like a group counseling session and it's, actually really cool."

They sat down on a park bench and were soon rewarded with the sight of a family of ducks, including eight little baby ducklings, waddling in front of them. The duck family continued down the hill and plopped, one by one, into the lake.

"Can you imagine having eight babies in your family?" Josh asked, watching the duck family swim by.

"No, I think I'd have no more than four," Amie replied. "But I guess I'll have whatever God has in mind for me."

"Four, wow…that's pretty brave."

"I know. Who knows? It may be that I won't have any. We'll have to see where life takes me. What about you?"

"Same. I would be open to a big family, but the bigger the family, the more expensive they are. I guess I'd better work on college before I worry about any of that."

"Where are you planning to go this fall?"

"I was accepted to UDub, Wazzu, and USC, but I actually like UDub's engineering program the best so I'm planning to go there."

"That's cool! At least you get to stay in the state, and the University of Washington is a really respected engineering school."

"Yeah. Those were the criteria I was looking at. I wanted to stay in state for college so we wouldn't have to deal with flights, and I wanted a school that was nationally recognized for their engineering program. But, make no mistake; I am really a WSU Coug deep down."

"I don't know Josh," Kendi teased. "I don't think a true Wazzu Coug could even consider being a Husky at UDub."

"Well, where are you going?"

"No idea. I still have two years to decide."

"Yeah, I guess you do. I always forget how young you are."

"Is that a compliment?"

"No, you just seem like a peer, not an underclassman."

"Upperclassman, now," Amie corrected as she looked at her phone to check the time. "I probably need to get back."

The two walked toward the parking lot. Josh waved as he got in his car. "See ya next time we work together!"

"See ya!" Amie called with a wave back.

As Josh drove away, Amie couldn't help thinking that some UW girl was going to be very lucky to be his girlfriend next year.

Judy Ann Koglin

CHAPTER EIGHT

Running Buddies

By the end of the week, all of the Guesthouse Girls' parents had left town.

Hope was sad to see her mom go, but she was focused on the future when they both might get to live in Chelan permanently.

Hope had been faithful with her morning runs when she wasn't working too early. On days when she had an early shift, she ran in the evenings.

Now that she was fairly certain that she was going to stay permanently in Chelan, she let her guard down a little and opened herself up to more friendships with local kids. Conner had told her about a group of runners from his school who got together to do track runs two mornings each week.

He invited her to come, assuring her she would not be the only girl. She agreed to stop by at some point.

This morning, she put on some athletic shoes and a t-shirt she received at basketball camp. She pulled her hair back in a ponytail, laced up her shoes, and headed to the high school. The road to the school was lined with a bunch of tall evergreen trees, and the sun shining off the hills was beautiful.

Conner had explained earlier that they ran on a course that began with a loop around the high school track, then traveled around the school campus, through the upper parking lot, and ended back at the track. In preparation, Hope stretched out in the field in the center of the track.

She thought about the fact this could very well be her track now…and her school. She had to admit that the thought gave her a shiver of excitement. She really hoped Uncle Joe's purchase of the sporting goods store worked out because her heart was 100% invested in this move, and if it fell through, both she and her mom would be devastated. Hope still could not believe that this beautiful town would actually be her home in the fall, and this group of kids would likely be her new friends.

One of the girls broke into her train of thought. She was medium height with shoulder length blonde hair and deep brown eyes. She was pretty but she had a look that made Hope think she had been through some rough experiences in her life. "Your name is Hope, right?"

"Yes," Hope answered, extending her hand.

"I'm Sierra. It's nice to meet you! I've seen you around with Amie Larson. Did you just move here?"

Since the purchase of the sporting goods hadn't gone through yet, there was nothing to talk about. She felt honest in saying, "I'm actually just here for the summer. My Uncle Joe owns Joe's Jet Skis and Boat Rentals, and I'm here to work for him."

"Oh, bummer. We're always hoping for more athletic girls at our school."

"Which sports do you play, Sierra?" Hope asked curiously.

"Soccer, basketball, and track. How about you?"

"Same."

"Okay, I will *pay* you to move here," Sierra joked. She gathered the other girls and introduced them to Hope. "Hope, this is Lily, Annalisa, and Maddie." Turning to the girls, she said, "Hope plays soccer and basketball and runs track. She's here just for the summer. I want her to move here."

Hope shook the other girls' hands.

Lily, a tall, friendly African-American girl smiled broadly and said, "Be careful, Hope. Sierra is relentless."

Hope grinned. "Fair warning."

Maddie, a medium-height redhead with freckles and short hair, asked Hope where she was from.

"I go to Lynnwood High. It's north of Seattle."

"Oh yeah, I've heard of it," Lily commented.

"So, shall we get running?" Annalisa, a short girl with dark hair and the muscles of a gymnast asked.

The girls warmed up as they jogged around the track, and Hope was excited to be hanging out with the girls who she may be spending the rest of high school with. She wished she could tell them that she was staying at the end of summer, but she knew she needed to wait.

When the run was finished, the girls invited Hope to get a coffee with them. Hope texted her uncle to see if it would be okay if she came in a little later than normal. He texted back that they had it covered until ten o' clock, and she could take her time.

◊ ◊◊◊ ◊

When they reached Brandon's Coffee and Bakeshop, Hope looked around, but she couldn't see Kendi working.

She was greeted by another girl, Reed.

"Hi, Hope!" Reed welcomed the group. "Kendi is coming a little later. What can we get for you?"

Hope ordered her drink, as did the four other girls. Once they got their beverages of choice, they sat at a table outside, and the gossip began.

"Annalisa, are you still mad at Brett?" Maddie asked.

"Yes. It's one thing to break up with me, but it's totally worse to do it via text! Just because he's heading off to college, he thought he could drop me like a rock," Annalisa sniffed.

Hope was assuming that they were talking about the Brett she knew because he was also a runner who had just graduated and was leaving for college soon. She was surprised and disappointed to hear that he would break up with a girl via a text message because he seemed so nice.

Hope really didn't like getting involved in gossip that wasn't her business, so she tried to change the subject. "Do all of you play soccer?" Hope asked the group.

"No, Lily and I run cross country, and Annalisa plays volleyball," Maddie stated. "We're all three-sport athletes. They kind of beg you to be when you go to a small school, so we're glad it's summer and that we get to have a break…except for camp."

"Yeah, I am missing soccer camp and basketball camp for my school," Hope reported. "My soccer coach said that as long as I kept in good condition this summer, he wouldn't penalize me for missing it, but my basketball coach was pretty mad."

"Coaches can get pretty intense about camp and practices," Sierra agreed. "I should know, my dad is the boys' soccer coach. He tries to get involved with the girls' team because I'm on it, but our coach makes him back off," she chuckled.

"When is your camp?" Hope asked nonchalantly.

"We are doing a short camp in Wenatchee this year. It starts in a few weeks," Sierra replied. Hope made a mental note in case the sale of the store went through and she could start practicing with the team.

"Volleyball camp is next week," Annalisa added. "It's in Bellevue this year."

"Football camp is coming up too, in Spokane," Sierra reported. "Bryan can't wait; all he talks about is how good the team is going to be--just in time for senior year."

"Bryan is Sierra's boyfriend," Lily told Hope. "They've been together forever."

"Off and on," Maddie reminded her. "Remember, he took me to homecoming freshman year to make her jealous!"

66

"Oh yeah! That's because he thought she liked Conner," Lily recalled.

"Well, I did like Conner, to be fair," Sierra explained. "Remember when Conner showed up to school at the beginning of our freshman year, and he'd gotten tall, lost his baby fat, was super tan, and was wearing the pink polo shirt?"

"Who could forget?" Lily recounted. "Every girl in the school wanted to date him, even the seniors," she laughed.

Hope waited expectantly hoping they would reveal more. She didn't have to wait long.

"He took Sierra to homecoming, but he really liked that girl who moved away," Annalisa remembered.

"Yeah? What was her name?" Lily asked.

"Isabelle," Maddie confirmed. "But remember, she turned out to be super mean and did all that cyber bullying. When the police caught her, their family ended up moving away."

Hope looked at Maddie in shock. "Who was she cyberbullying?" she asked.

"Anyone that she felt was a threat to her relationship with Conner," Lily explained.

"I guess I was her first victim," Sierra revealed. "She got some risqué pictures of some other girl and posted them on a fake account with my name.

67

I knew it was her that did it and my parents reported her to the police. It was humiliating but everyone who knew me could tell that it wasn't me because the picture was obviously a different person."

"Then she started picking on another girl for no reason. Such a bully! The police built their case against her and the FBI got involved. They reached some sort of plea agreement," Sierra reported.

"So, in the end, Conner lost out and he didn't end up with her or with me because Bryan and I got back together," Sierra stated.

"Who's dating him now?" Hope couldn't help but ask.

"He's been lying low lately. He's gone to Sadie Hawkins a couple times and Homecoming when girls ask him, but I don't think he's really had a girlfriend since the Isabelle debacle," Maddie said.

"Speaking of Homecoming, I really hope Cody asks me this year. It's our senior year and my last chance to go with him," Lily stated.

"It's a long time until homecoming. You should focus on something else," Sierra advised.

Annalisa looked at her phone, "Yikes! I gotta jet! I told my mom I would be home by 9:30 this morning."

"I need to go, too," Hope agreed.

"Me, too," the other girls agreed, and they dispersed at the parking lot.

◊ ◊◊◊ ◊

Hope hurried into work just when several potential customers walked up. She immediately jumped into helping Uncle Joe with the rush and didn't have time to mentally process everything that the girls discussed that morning at the coffee shop. The day stayed busy, and she worked late to make up for coming in behind schedule.

When she finally got home that night, she pulled out a leftover enchilada from the fridge and microwaved it.

Nobody seemed to be around, so she stretched out on the couch and thought about her day. She thought it was interesting to think about how Conner was kind of short and chubby in middle school, and he'd transformed in the summer before his freshman year. She thought about this new group of girls: Sierra, Maddie, Lily, and Annalisa. They could very well be her friend group in the coming year…not quite as good as The Guesthouse Girls, but at least she would have some friends to stay in shape with. That was progress. Unfortunately, they would all be seniors in the fall. Hopefully there were some nice girls in the junior class, too.

◊ ◊◊◊ ◊

Over on Main Street, Emma had spent the day working in the back room of the store. Mr. Femley was showing her how to take inventory and how to determine when items needed to be purchased. Emma soaked in all the information.

Mr. Femley loved to have someone so passionate about the business to train. Emma asked questions not to just learn a task, but to really get an understanding of the thought process that went into the ordering. Sometimes, she made suggestions about what they could do to get more sales. My Femley was thrilled with her enthusiasm and allowed her to try some of her ideas, even when he was pretty sure he had tried them before without success. He figured it was all part of her learning process.

Today, Emma's idea was to make little coupons and have hotels give them to their customers when they checked in. The coupon would encourage them to make a bigger purchase, not just get a bottle of sunscreen for $8.99. Her suggestion was to have the coupon be for 10% off a $25 order, or 15% off a $50 order. Since many of their receipts were for about $19 unless they were buying clothes, Emma was hoping to increase the average ticket for people buying just small things.

Because Mr. Femley gave her permission to find one business that would try the coupon idea, Emma went down the block and talked to the front desk representative of a nearby budget motel. They agreed to use the coupon if it was branded as a special deal valid only for their guests this week.

Emma ran back to Femley's, whipped out a simple coupon on the computer in the back room, printed off 30 of them, cut them out, and delivered them to the hotel manager in less than an hour. The manager agreed to hand them to each incoming guest that week. Emma crossed her fingers and hoped the idea would be successful.

Mr. Femley instructed the cashiers in his store that the coupon was coming out and told them to run a duplicate receipt and attach the coupon to it so they could analyze the results when the promotion was done.

Feeling satisfied, Emma knew all they could do was wait and see if any of the coupons showed up this week.

Emma went back to her inventory duties in the back room and came upon a pile of brightly colored plastic bins. "What are these?" she asked.

Mr. Femley shrugged. "They are just some plastic baskets that a vendor gave us one time. We used to use them for displays."

Emma suddenly lit up. "They just gave me an idea!"

"Oh no, another one of Emma's crazy ideas," Tricia teased as she entered the back room to grab more sodas to stock their refrigerated cooler.

"What if we made rainy day baskets for kids?" Emma continued, undeterred. "We can fill them with Uno playing cards, activity books, microwave popcorn, and other stuff? We'd keep them back here. When there's rainy weather in the forecast, we can bring them out with a sign and sell them."

"I like that idea," Mr. Femley replied thoughtfully. "How about if you make up three of them, and next time we have a rainy day, we can try out the idea? Keep the price between $15 and $20. I don't think people will spend much more."

"Okay! I'll get a few of them made," Emma said.

Emma eagerly dove into the task, making three different baskets, each around the suggested price, and wrapping them up with cellophane and a bow.

Mr. Femley nodded his approval. "That ought to brighten the day of kids who can't swim!"

Emma finished her inventory duties and went home excited and satisfied because she got to use her creative ideas to hopefully help the store. She couldn't wait to see if any of her coupons were redeemed in the week ahead.

CHAPTER NINE

Meeting Duke

One day at work, Rachel Brandon approached Kendi. "We are going to be taking our boat out next Thursday, and I was wondering if you and your friends from The Guesthouse would want to go, if they are available?"

"Can we all fit?" Kendi asked innocently, picturing a small fishing boat.

Rachel laughed. "Actually, the boat can fit 12 people, although it is more comfortable with ten. Mark's dad bought it before he died. We kept it, and occasionally rent it out to friends to help pay for moorage. Tell the girls that if they want to come, they need to get the whole day off because we'll leave around nine and go up to Stehekin for lunch. I'll call Nola to see if she wants to go, too."

Kendi was so excited. She kept hearing the word "Stehekin," but she didn't really know what it was. She made a mental note to research it online, so she knew what she was talking about when she told her friends.

When Kendi got off at 2:30, she changed into her swimsuit, applied sunscreen, and threw on a casual summer dress. She filled her insulated water bottle with filtered water from the fridge and placed it in her colorful tote bag along with her neatly folded fluffy yellow beach towel. She added a mystery book she had been reading, as well as a devotional book she had received from Aunty Nola at her baptism. Once she plunked her phone into the bag, she was ready to go to the lake.

Kendi walked a short way to get to her favorite place to relax. Because of her fair skin, she had to be careful not to burn, so her preferred spot was shaded by an old oak tree. Sometimes, she liked to sit with her back resting on the tree as she read. She occasionally looked up when she completed a chapter and saw a sailboat floating by on the lake.

Today, Kendi settled into her spot and decided to start relaxing by reading her devotional book. Christianity was still very new to her, and this journal gave her a place to read scripture and write down her thoughts.

The passage today was from Acts 7. It was part of the speech that Stephen gave before he was martyred. The speech outlined some of the history of the Jewish nation. Kendi decided that she wanted more information, so she pulled out her phone and looked up Acts 7 in her Bible app. The chapter gave a lot of information, starting with Abraham being called out of Mesopotamia. Kendi wanted to know more. She decided to talk to Aunty Nola about the best way to learn.

She wrote in her journal: *"Stephen was a brave and intelligent man. He was under a lot of pressure and stress, and he was still able to give an organized history of his people. He knew that what he said would probably end up getting him killed, but he chose to say it anyway. His faith in God was crazy strong. I wonder if he thought that God would rescue him from death by striking the bad men with lightening? It kind of seems like he knew he would die, and he wasn't afraid because he kind of got in their faces and told them off after the history lesson. I don't know if I would do that."*

Kendi put down her pen and decided to stretch out in the sun for awhile and relax. She spread the towel out and closed her eyes. She prayed silently that God would help her understand the Bible because a lot of things in it were confusing to her. After her prayer, she drifted off to sleep.

75

An hour later, she was awakened by the sound of a dog barking nearby. He was a beautiful white Maltese held on the leash by a young blonde woman and a man with light brown hair who looked like he could be her husband or boyfriend. Kendi thought the three of them would make a cute photo. She wondered if they were locals, or if they were here on vacation.

Kendi summoned up her courage, got up, walked over to where they were situated, and asked if it would be okay if she petted their beautiful dog.

The woman said, "Oh, yes! Duke is really friendly."

Kendi reached out to him and petted him. Duke loved the attention and rolled onto his back to get a belly rub. Kendi played with him for a few minutes while the couple laughed at Duke's funny antics.

The lady asked Kendi if she went to Chelan High.

"No," Kendi replied. "I'm from Redmond, but I'm staying at The Guesthouse this summer. Do you know where that is?"

"Indeed, I do," the young lady responded with a smile. "My little sister Elizabeth actually lived at The Guesthouse with Aunty Nola one summer about ten years ago when I was 18," she revealed.

"My friend and I came up to here visit her. We booked a room in a cheap motel for two nights. We heard they were having a street dance that weekend and we wanted to stay an extra night, so we bought a tent from Craigslist and asked someone if we could set up our tent in their grass for ten bucks. Turns out, the homeowners had a son, and we ended up hitting it off. So, my friend and I got to stay and go to the street dance, and I ended up eventually marrying the son," she revealed, pointing to the man who was with her.

Kendi turned, wide-eyed, to this man in question. "It was *you*?" she squealed.

"Guilty as charged," he said, grinning. "She looked so cute at the street dance with messy hair and sunburned cheeks, so I threw caution to the wind and asked her to dance. I guess she liked me, too, because she's still around."

"Oh, that's a great story! What happened to your sister who lived at The Guesthouse?" Kendi asked.

"She ended up marrying a pastor and moving to Nebraska. I don't understand the Nebraska thing, but I think they are happy."

Kendi stood up. "Well, I'd better get going home. I'm glad I ran into you. By the way, my name is Kendi, and I work at Brandons' Coffee and Bakeshop."

"Nice to meet you, Kendi. I'm Lynsie, and this is Christopher. Maybe we'll see you at Brandon's sometime?"

"Sounds good!" Kendi said, giving Duke's fur a final rub. She waved goodbye to the three of them, folded up her towel, put everything back in her bag, and headed for home.

She reflected on Lynsie and Christopher's chance meeting at the street dance as she made her way back to The Guesthouse. *How romantic,* she thought, *to think they're still together and even married now with a puppy. I wonder who I will marry."*

Her thoughts wandered to Ryan, and she felt a little shiver. He was so handsome and charming, with his dark hair and warm smile. She couldn't help feeling special when he paid attention to her. However, she knew he was friendly and that he had that effect on a lot of people, including Emma. Something inside her told her that she'd better guard her heart against Ryan.

She consciously turned her thoughts to Ben. He was equally good-looking with a tall, athletic-looking body, long blonde hair like a surfer, and a great tan. He seemed like he also could be a heartbreaker as well, but she was just good friends with him at this point, so as long as they kept it at that level, her heart would be safe.

If I find my husband in Chelan like Lynsie did, it will have to be when I am older, she decided.

◊ ◊◊◊ ◊

When Kendi got home, she was greeted by Aunty Nola and Emma. Aunty Nola told her that Rachel had called to invite her to the boating day.

"Are you going to come?" Kendi asked.

"I think I will. When Garry was alive, we used to go up to Stehekin every now and then, but I haven't gotten a chance to go much since then. Our ladies' ministry had a retreat there a few years ago, and it was just gorgeous. It is always wonderful to spend time with God out in nature," she said, smiling at the thought.

"Emma, you're invited, too," Kendi assured her. "So are Amie and Hope."

"I know! I stopped by the coffee shop this afternoon, and Ben told me. I told him to save me a seat next to him or Ryan in case I get seasick. But then again, the last think I'd want to do is get sick next to one of those boys!" she laughed.

Kendi was surprised to find that she had a little glint of jealously when she heard Emma's comment. She reminded herself that Ben and Ryan weren't just her friends, and they were allowed to have lots of friends besides her, maybe even girlfriends.

"I'm definitely getting off work that day," Emma reported. "I already asked for it off, and Mr. Femley agreed because we have enough staff to cover for me."

"George is very accommodating, from what I've heard," Aunty Nola commented as she turned the oven on and added some peeled potatoes to the roast she had prepared in the pan.

"He really is! I just love him," Emma confessed. She looked out the window and saw Hope coming up the porch steps.

As soon as Hope got into the door, Emma blurted, "Hi, Hope! We're all invited to go boating with Ben's family a week from Thursday if you can get off work."

Hope grinned. "That was a little fast, Emma. I'm not sure I heard it all."

Kendi and Nola also smiled.

"Rachel Brandon invited us to go to Stehekin with her family on their boat a week from Thursday. It'll be an all-day trip, so we all need to get the day off from work in order to go," Emma said slowly, enunciating every word.

"Oh, that sounds great! I love going up there!" Amie said cheerfully as she entered the kitchen. The others were startled by her sudden entrance; she had been so quiet that nobody had noticed her arrive. Amie texted the kitchen manager at the resort to make sure her request reached him right away before he put out the next schedule.

"I'll see if I can go," Hope responded. "I haven't done a lot of boating, even though I work for a boat rental place, so I don't know if I would get seasick." Hope looked at Aunty Nola because she knew she'd have a solution to her concern.

"Don't worry, dear. We will bring Dramamine and ginger candy, and we can take one at the first sign of nausea."

"Should be fun!" Amie predicted. "The Brandons are an awesome family."

"What is Stehekin?" Kendi asked. She had been meaning to research it on her phone, but she hadn't gotten around to it.

Aunty Nola added some carrots to the pan and put the roast in the oven. "Stehekin is a charming town about two hours north of us by boat. It is a lovely little community, and people love to go out there to get way from it all. Rachel Brandon said we would plan to eat lunch there and spend a few hours enjoying the town. Oh, by the way, girls, the roast will be done in a little over an hour, so make sure you are here by 6:40."

"I'll be here," Emma said resolutely.

"Me, too," the other girls chorused.

Emma and Hope went upstairs to respond to texts.

After the other girls had filtered out, Kendi asked Aunty Nola, "Do you need any help?"

"I think the cooking is done; if you could set the table, that would be great," Aunty Nola responded.

Kendi set out the woven placemats and arranged the five plates and silverware around the table, added the salt and paper shakers and the butter plate and knife, then went outside and sat on the back porch with Aunty Nola and Amie. She told them about her time in the park and reading about Stephen in her devotional.

"Stephen was the first recorded martyr in the New Testament, if you don't count John the Baptist," Aunty Nola began.

"What does that mean? I've only heard that word use negatively, like, 'Don't be a martyr,'" Kendi explained.

"A martyr is someone who dies for their faith," Nola explained.

"Why was he willing to do that? Why didn't he just be quiet and not talk about his faith, so he could keep living and keep doing good?" Kendi asked.

"He felt like the things he had to say needed to be said," Amie answered.

"Not only that, but the Bible also tells us in Matthew 5 not to hide our light, but let it shine," Nola added.

"The Bible also tells us if we deny Him before men, He will deny us before God," Amie said soberly.

"Oh, that's scary," Kendi said. "I'm glad the killing of Christians ended a long time ago."

"Actually, in many other countries, Christians are routinely persecuted and even killed for their faith, even today." Nola reported. "Even their families turn away from them if they receive Christ as their Savior."

"Wow, I had no idea that still went on in the 21st century."

"Yes, it still does, and it will likely continue until Christ comes back." Nola stated.

"When I was reading my Bible, I realized that it's sometimes really hard to understand," Kendi admitted. "I think I need to go to a class."

"Come with me when I teach Sunday school!" Amie suggested. "I teach four- and five-year-olds once every few weeks. It sounds juvenile, but I actually learn a lot when I teach them."

"I'll definitely come," Kendi said. "I'm probably about the same level as they are, so I think it'd be fun."

"Ok, let's see when I am on the schedule again." Amie said, consulting her phone. "Ha, we're in luck! I'm on for this week."

"Good! I'm excited for this!" Kendi exclaimed.

CHAPTER TEN

Stehekin Excursion

The girls counted down the days until their boat trip. They planned their outfits, researched the town online, and decided what they would do when they got there.

When the day arrived, the girls got ready, and Aunty Nola drove them to the marina where the Brandon's boat was docked. Ben had told Kendi that this boat did not just belong to his dad, but also to his Uncle Rob and their family who lived in Portland. He said that they would be coming to town later this summer and would probably be using the boat a lot when they were here.

When they arrived at the boat, Mark and Rachel were there to greet them. A few minutes later, a slightly disheveled Ben and Cody joined them.

Rachel told the kids that she would sit next to her husband, who was sitting in the captain's position; Nola could sit by her, and the rest of them could sit wherever they could find a spot. She showed them where the lifejackets were kept. She also said that they had plenty of drinks on ice and to feel free to grab one without asking if they were thirsty. She also showed them where to dump any trash they might generate.

Mark then asked who would like to water ski or wakeboard. Several hands went up.

"Okay," Mark said, "let's go upriver a ways first and wait for it to get a little hotter. Then, we can do some skiing and wakeboarding."

The morning air was still a little chilly as they whizzed through the water. The four girls wrapped themselves in their beach towels and huddled together in the bow of the boat. Cody and Ben had wisely worn sweatshirts and were stretched out comfortably in seats in the rear.

After a half hour of driving, Mark stopped the boat and said, "Who's first?"

Ben and Cody rock-paper-scissored to see which one would go first, and Cody's scissors beat out Ben's paper.

"Pick your poison," Mark offered, pointing to the wakeboards and skis.

"Wakeboard," Cody answered, carefully extracting it from the overhead storage where it was attached. Ben grabbed the rope and made sure it was untangled as Cody sat on the edge of the boat and squished his size 13 feet into the boots attached to the board. When he was ready, he carefully lifted his long legs with the board attached and pivoted his lanky body around so the board would not come in contact with the side of the boat. He hung onto the rope as he slowly sank into the cool water.

"Brrr! Still frigid," said Cody, shivering.

Rachel held up an orange flag indicating they had someone in the water, even though they were the only boat around.

Ben fed the rope out as Mark slowly taxied the boat to make the rope taut. Cody crouched his body, pulled back his arms, and prepared for a jolt of speed.

Cody yelled, "Hit it!" and the boat took off, propelling him to his feet.

Rachel lowered the flag, and everyone kept their eyes fixed on Cody as he deftly navigated the wake with picture-perfect jumps. Noting the girls' attention, he did a few tricks like flipping his body 180 degrees by moving his hips so his left foot went from the back position to the front position.

He did this again to reverse the rotation and got cheers from the people in the boat. He ran out of tricks that he was good at and didn't want to risk embarrassing himself in front of the group of girls, so he did a few more jumps and then dropped the rope and waved.

Rachel snapped the orange flag into the air and Mark circled back so Cody could grab the rope. Ben hauled the rope back into the boat with Cody coming along for the ride. Cody let go of the rope, climbed the ladder on the end of the boat, and drip dried while standing on the top rung.

"Ben, are you next?" Mark asked. "Let's let the girls wait until it warms up a little more."

Ben took the board from Cody, slipped his feet in, and lowered himself into the water.

Rachel asked Amie if she would spot for her so she could get some snacks out. Amie accepted the orange flag and held it up until Mark started the boat and propelled Ben out of the water.

"He's heavier than last year," Mark complained.

"That's because of all the lifting he has been doing at the gym," Rachel laughed. "He's put on 15 pounds of muscle this year."

It was getting too loud to hear anything over the sound of the motor, but that didn't matter at all to Ben, who could wakeboard even better than Cody.

He looked effortless as he made high arching jumps. He signaled his dad that he was going to try to do a front flip. Mark shrugged because he wasn't sure if the boat had enough power to enable him to do that trick since there were so many passengers. However, he still pushed the accelerator to provide more power, and Ben was able to complete the flip. The ladies all cheered wildly, and Mark and Rachel nodded in admiration. Ben dropped the rope and waved, and Amie raised the orange flag while Cody pulled him in.

"Hey, man, why'd you have to show me up in front of all the ladies?" Cody jokingly complained.

"I didn't think you would be able to pull that off with so much weight in the boat," his dad admitted. "I thought it'd be an epic fail."

"I wasn't sure, either," Ben confessed, "but I wanted to see if I could still do it."

"Great job, son," Rachel said, handing him a packet of trail mix. She passed the packets around so others could grab some, too.

"Rachel? Nola? Did either of you want to go?" Mark asked.

"I might ski this afternoon on the way back from Stehekin if that would work," Aunty Nola said gamely.

"I'm not feeling it today," Rachel declared. "Do any of you girls want to try?"

Hope had been dying to get a chance since she had never done any water sports before, with the exception of taking her uncle's watercraft out for a spin, so she volunteered to go first.

Ben and Cody were only too glad to help get her outfitted in a life vest and show her what to do.

Hope seemed to pick up the technique readily after just a few questions, so she lowered herself into the water and got in position.

"Yell 'hit it' when you're ready," Ben called.

"Hit it!" Hope called firmly.

Mark accelerated, and she rose into position.

"I've never seen anyone get up on their first attempt," Rachel gushed.

"Especially someone who has never even skied," Mark agreed.

"I never even taught her how to cross the wake because I didn't think she'd get that far," Ben said.

The girls were cheering her on, and Cody and Ben were trying to coach her from the rear of the boat. Another boat sped by, and Ben could see that Hope would soon be affected by their wake. He motioned for her to bend her knees to absorb the impact of the choppy water. She recognized what he was trying to tell her and bent her knees just in time, managing to stay upright until the water was flat again. She got bored staying where she was, so she experimented, leaning her body so she could float way to the right of the boat and then back to the position she started. Then she waved and dropped the rope, and they pulled her back in.

She was greeted with wild applause and positive comments.

When she was still in the water, and Amie had the orange flag raised, Ben asked Hope why she didn't try to cross the wake.

"I wanted to get instructions first," Hope told him. "If I did it wrong, I'd probably crash and burn and I didn't want to embarrass myself."

"Okay! Let's try that again." This time, Mark gave her clear instructions on how to navigate the wake. After his briefing, he once again taxied the boat and got Hope upright in the water. This time, she lifted her left foot and zoomed over the wake. She repositioned her weight, crossed the wake, and ended up back where she started. She got the hang of it and started doing it faster.

The boys could tell that she was thinking of jumping the wake. "Go for it!" the boys yelled.

She bent her knees and did her first jump. When she landed, her board caught the wake. She crashed, and her feet popped out of her boots.

Emma and Kendi were concerned about Hope.

"Don't worry," Amie assured them. Crashing is normal. I'm surprised this is the first crash today."

"It was the first crash, wasn't it?" Rachel said. "I guess the boys were being extra careful trying not to crash in front of you, and Hope is just a natural."

Hope wanted to try to land a jump again, so she went out and landed four great beginner jumps before she waved, dropped the rope and waited while the boat swung around to retrieve her.

"You can bet I'm not going to follow that," Emma declared.

"Oh, come on, Emma," Ben coaxed, putting an arm around her encouragingly. "We'll put you on the kid-sized board, and you'll do fine."

"I use the kid-sized board, too," Amie responded so Emma would know that Ben was being serious. "It works better for our height."

"Can you wakeboard like that?" Emma asked.

"Actually, Hope is already at my level, and I've wakeboarded for several years," Amie admitted.

"She'll probably catch us up to us by the end of the day," Ben predicted. "How about you, Dad? Are you ready to go?"

"Yeah. I'd better get out there before Hope gets better than me." Mark got up and grabbed a large life jacket, and Rachel slid into his seat to drive.

Mark slipped on the boots and got into position. Amie assigned flag duty to Kendi, leaned back, and relaxed in the now-warm sun.

Mr. Brandon was really good, even better than Ben. He did a couple of flips and another trick where he flipped while he was doing a 360-degree turn.

When he was finished and returned to his place in the boat, he admitted that wakeboarding actually tired him out these days. "I'm getting to be an old man," he joked.

"You better not be, because that would make me an old lady," Rachel retorted.

"I'm hungry," Ben spoke up, "and I bet Cody is too!" Cody nodded and rubbed his stomach.

"Okay! Full speed to Stehekin for some lunch," Mark said.

He accelerated the engine, and they sped up to the northwest.

◊ ◊◊◊ ◊

When they arrived, they docked at one of the available slips. Cody and Ben jumped out, secured the ropes on the cleats, and offered a hand to each of the ladies to help them out.

"Make sure you take your valuables with you," Rachel warned. "We have had stuff taken before, so I am always careful now."

"Okay, everyone, you can get lunch at one of the food trucks; they are all delicious. When walking around town, you must stay in groups of at least two people at all times. Be back here in two hours. If we are all back sooner, we'll leave earlier," Rachel announced.

The four girls started out together. The boys were another group, and Mr. and Mrs. Brandon walked around with Aunty Nola.

Emma told the girls about the coupon she had designed for Femley's General Store that the budget hotel gave out to their guests: "We had five coupons come back this week. Four of them were for just over $50, and one was for $25. Mr. Femley said he predicted that we would only get one at the most, and he was really pleased with the response rate. He said I could expand the coupon project to other hotels. Do you think the resort would do it, Amie?"

"I don't know! We could ask," Amie promised.

The girls entered the first store to look around. It was just what Kendi would have expected in this charming town. It had exposed wood beams and racks of tourist items such as hats, stuffed animals, and postcards. A variety of different Stehekin-themed t-shirts were available to buy. The store also had candy, drinks, and groceries for locals.

The girls thoroughly enjoyed sifting through all the merchandise, looking for souvenirs.

In the meantime, the boys, who had been here many times before, headed to a nearby park after they had consumed hamburgers with onion rings. Ben decided to shoot a few hoops to pass the time while the others finished lunch.

There were some smaller boys playing basketball. One little boy came up to the "bigger kids" – after asking his mom seated nearby if it was okay - and asked if they could be the coaches since they were big.

Cody and Ben liked that idea, and each of the "coaches" took their "team" aside to discuss strategy. Ben taught his kids an easy offense that he'd learned when he was in middle school. Cody talked to his kids about the importance of staying with your man to make sure each person was being guarded.

The teams assembled in the middle, and Cody made each of his little team members match up with a guy from the other team so they knew who they were guarding. Ben conducted a jump ball and the little guys attempted to play a basketball game. After a while Ben whistled and called a time out. "What did you need, Coach?" one of the kids asked earnestly.

Ben had to laugh at being called "Coach". "Okay, guys, remember the offense I taught you? Now, we are going to use it." The boys gave him blank stares, so he again showed each of the boys what to do during the play. "Put your right hand in the center," Ben instructed. "When I count to three, you're going to say 'Break' and pull your arms back. Ready? One…two…three…"

"Break!" his team yelled.

Cody's team wanted to do the break as well, so Cody showed them how.

Then, the game resumed. The offense was never mastered, and the kids didn't always guard their man, but everyone had fun and possibly even learned a little bit. One of the kids' moms, who was sitting on a bench watching, complimented Cody and Ben on how well they worked with the kids.

"We really came to the park to see if we could get in on a pick-up game," Cody explained, "but this was fun, too."

Ben nodded. "Let's head back to the main street and get snow cones."

The boys found the snow cone truck and saw that the adults had already been there and were still consuming their treats. Ben ordered half lime, half grapefruit, and Cody ordered half pina colada, half root beer. Ben asked where the girls were.

"One of the craft shops has a place where people can make their own jewelry. I think some of them are making bracelets," Nola offered.

"Oh, of course!" chorused the boys.

"Why didn't we think of that, Cody?" Ben laughed.

"I know! You could've made me a necklace that matched my eyes," Cody batted his eyes.

"All right, you two," Rachel chuckled. "Why don't you head back the boat, and we can hurry the girls along?" Rachel suggested. She and Aunty Nola walked to the shop just as the girls were coming out the door.

"What did you make?" Aunty Nola asked.

The girls showed off their creations. Emma's bracelet had red and white beads with a heart charm in the middle, and Kendi's bracelet had gold, olive green, and brown hues for fall. Hope's bracelet was a black elastic strand with the four letters HOPE strung in the middle. She figured it was a double meaning...both her name and the concept of hope. Amie had made two bracelets because she couldn't choose between all the pretty colors. Her first one was iridescent pink, bright violet, and light blue, and the second one was Seahawks colors, lime green and navy blue. On that one, she had attached a little football charm.

97

After showing Aunty Nola and Rachel their creations, they tucked them safely away.

By the time they reached the dock, it was really hot out, and everyone was feeling uncomfortable and a little sweaty. They were glad when the boat's engine started running so they could be cooled by the breeze.

◊ ◊◊◊ ◊

After a few minutes, Mark stopped the boat.

"You're up, Amie," he announced. He pulled down the kid-sized wakeboard and Ben gave her a small life jacket. She slipped into the boot after Ben put some foamy soap onto her little foot.

"I feel like Cinderella trying to squeeze my foot in here," Amie pointed out.

"Yeah, you're kind of in between the kid size and the adult size, but the smaller-sized boards are easier to do tricks with, if you wanted to," Mark explained.

"My only trick is to stay up," Amie laughed. It did take her a few tries to get up, but Mr. Brandon took the blame because he was accelerating too fast for her size.

"What are you, 90 pounds?" asked Mr. Brandon.

"No, 100 pounds!" she said proudly from the water.

"Okay, Amie, let's try this again."

He hit the accelerator gently at her command, and she rose gracefully and glided across the wake like a swan. She didn't do any jumps or tricks, but she looked elegant with what she did. Even when she was finished and dropped the rope, she gave them the pageant wave, barely moving her arm and just twisting her wrist.

Emma knew they would tell her to go next, and she was apprehensive. She looked at Kendi with panic in her eyes. "I just know I'm going to be terrible. I really don't want to embarrass myself in front of the boys. Do you think I can bow out?" she asked.

"If you really don't want to do it, I'll have your back," Kendi whispered.

"I really don't...not in front of this many people," Emma confirmed.

"Okay," Kendi whispered back. She then turned her attention to Aunty Nola. "Hey, Aunty Nola, you wanted to ski, right?"

"Oh, yes. I was going to ski, but I wanted to let you girls have a chance."

"Emma's not going to go today, and I can go after you," Kendi suggested.

"Okay! I'll get geared up. How cold was the water, Amie?" she asked as Amie was drying off.

"Not too bad, really."

"Okay, I'll give it a whirl…skiing that is, not wakeboarding," Aunty Nola corrected her response.

Mr. Brandon secured the kid-sized wakeboard back on the overhead tower bar, got the skis down, and gave them to Ben so he could help Aunty Nola. She leaned on the edge of the boat, and he helped soap up her feet and assisted her with her graceful, straight-legged descent into the water. The teenagers were all surprised how agile she was.

"Brrr, that is cold!" she cried.

"It'll seem warmer in a minute," Ben assured her.

He threw her the rope, which she caught in one hand. She crouched down, waited for the boat to taxi until the rope was pulled taut, and then yelled, "Hit it!"

The boat pulled her slim figure up, and she surprised everyone with her expertise on the skis. She deftly handled the wake. At one point, she indicated that she was going to drop a ski, so she slipped her left foot out of its ski boot, put it behind her right foot, and skied for a minute on just one ski. She quickly waved goodbye because she knew that the boat would have to turn around and retrieve the other ski, so it wouldn't become a hazard in case another boat came by.

When she came back onto the boat, everyone cheered.

"Aunty Nola, I had no idea you could do that!" Rachel exclaimed.

"Me neither," Aunty Nola said with a wink. "I haven't skied for years!"

"You must have been phenomenal back in the day," Mr. Brandon remarked.

"Well, remember, I grew up on this lake, and really, the only things to do were swimming and boating. There was no internet or video games. My girlfriend and I would put on our bathing suits, lie out in the sun on the docks, and wait for a couple guys to come by who needed a spotter. We would agree to come as long as we could ski with them."

"That sounds risky for young girls," Rachel said.

"It was the sixties," Nola explained. "It was a much different time. Still, my mother would not have liked it if she knew what we were doing when we said we were tanning. We did come back with a tan, though!"

The girls looked at Aunty Nola in a new light. First, they found out she was a rocking good skier, even though she hadn't skied for a decade–AND she was 70 years old–and now they found out that she would go down to the dock and hitch a boat ride with boys so that she could ski with them.

They had to laugh. What other fun secrets might Aunty Nola have?

Kendi knew in a few minutes that they would want her to try. She was a little apprehensive, but she also wanted to master this skill. She was determined to give it a go, but she wasn't going to suggest it until someone else did.

It didn't take long. "Kendi, it's your turn," Ben reminded her...and everybody.

Well, now or never, she thought, looking around for the driest-looking life jacket.

"Here's one," Rachel said, lifting the seat cushion beneath her and pulling out a blue and black one that hadn't been used yet. "Use this jacket, Kendi."

Kendi wrapped the dry life jacket around her as if it was armor against the cold water in which she would soon be immersed. She made her way to the back of the boat where Ben and Cody were preparing to soap up her feet.

Awkward, she thought.

However, it would probably be more awkward to refuse their help, so she submitted to the soaping and subsequent shoving of her feet into the wakeboard boots. She knew what came next, and she was not excited. However, as she stood in the sun roasting with the life jacket and boots on, she thought the cold water might not be so bad.

She straightened out her legs and pivoted her bottom like she saw the others do, and she dropped into the water with gritted teeth and tensed shoulders. When she started to submerge, she realized it really wasn't all that cold.

Now she had to remember what all the instructions were, so she whispered them back to herself: "Tuck my body together, bend my arms, hold the rope handle with two hands, lean my head back, and wait until the rope is taut...then say, 'hit it.'"

She did it mostly right, and after a few botched attempts, she was able to be vertical in the water. It felt good to glide across the lake on the board. She felt like she was flying 90 miles per hour, but she found out later it was only about 20 miles per hour.

She knew the next step was to attempt to cross the wake. It looked daunting. She remembered the instructions she'd heard them give Hope, which they were trying to yell and pantomime to her now. She tried to shift her weight and glide over the wake, but unfortunately, she caught an edge and wiped out spectacularly.

She had a moment of panic as she was hurtling through the air, landed, and briefly sank in the water, but she popped right up and saw the boat in the process of turning around to retrieve her.

She realized that the board was no longer attached to her, so she looked around, saw it, and swam toward it.

She snatched it, hung on for dear life, and heard Ben yelling, "Grab the rope!" Unfortunately, she missed the rope, and it was too far to grab, so Ben called out, "Just wait, we're coming back!"

The boat circled again, and Kendi was ready. She had the wakeboard in one hand and grabbed the rope with the other, and she let Ben pull her back to the safety of the boat. Cody retrieved the wakeboard from her, and Ben helped her onboard.

Ben had his back to everyone else, shielding Kendi from the others. He asked her if she wanted to try again, knowing what the answer would be.

She shook her head "no."

Ben unzipped and removed her life jacket, then wrapped a towel around her now-shivering body. He gave her a big hug, even though her arms were wrapped up like a mummy in the towel. He cupped her chin, lifted up her head, complete with her chattering teeth, and said, "Kendi, you're so cute all cold and wet! You did great getting up. Next time we come out, you'll cross the wake, no problem."

Kendi spirits were brightened by Ben's kind words and actions.

She stumbled to the front of the boat where she was greeted by her buddies. Amie reminded her that a lot of people aren't able to get up on a wakeboard on their first trip out, so she was far ahead of many people.

Emma thanked Kendi for covering for her so she wouldn't be pressured to go because se knew she would have done even worse than Kendi did. Those words weren't particularly comforting, but Kendi knew what she meant. Hope couldn't say much because she had just gone out and killed it and it was also her first time. She did put her arm around Kendi and gave her a side hug. Kendi appreciated the silent gesture.

After that, each of the boys and Mr. Brandon took turns, then Nola and Hope also decided to have another go at it. Rachel Brandon decided that she wanted to go as well because it was getting so hot sitting in the boat. Kendi stretched out to the best of her ability and let the warm sun dry her off and take the chill away.

◊ ◊◊◊ ◊

When they reached the docks back in Chelan, nobody felt like walking home, so Aunty Nola, Hope and Amie squeezed into the back seat of the Brandon's car, and Emma and Kendi got a ride from Cody and Ben.

When they reached The Guesthouse, they all thanked the Brandons for the great day. All five of The Guesthouse occupants stretched out on their beds and fell fast asleep, missing dinner.

Kendi woke up at 7 p.m., and it took a minute for her to realize that it was evening and not morning. She staggered groggily down the stairs. Hope and Aunty Nola were sitting in the kitchen drinking iced tea and talking. Kendi joined them, hoping she wasn't interrupting a private conversation.

"Did you want some iced tea, my dear?" Aunty Nola asked.

"Yes, please," Kendi replied as Nola poured her a tall glass. "Are the others up?"

"Yes. Amie and Emma woke up about ten minutes before you, and they were going to walk to the park to watch the sunset. They should be back in a little while, I imagine."

"We were just talking about how God makes us all so different, but despite our differences and really because of them, we can live harmoniously," Aunty Nola told the two girls. "Just think about it. If you want your plumbing fixed, you call someone who is good at plumbing. You don't call someone who is a math tutor. However, if your son needs help in math, you probably wouldn't call the plumber; you'd call a guy who was good at math.

Just like you girls each have your own passions and things you excel at, you are all different from each other, but together, you are so good for each other."

Hope looked to Kendi and said, "I am so happy to have you, Amie, and Emma. You have literally changed my life and helped me to open up and not be so closed off. I always tend to think that people won't like me because our family doesn't have money, so I tend to hide behind my athletics and think if I just run faster or shoot more goals, I will be good enough."

Kendi was shocked by this rare glimpse into Hope's closely guarded psyche. "Oh, Hope, I had no idea you felt this way," she shared with her friend. "You're a lovely person, and if anyone judges you based on how much money they think you have or don't have, then they're missing out on knowing the amazing you."

"That is what I have been telling her all summer," Aunty Nola confirmed.

"Most people in the world look at the outward appearance like beauty, talent and wealth, but God looks at the heart. He wants His people to be kind and good to everybody, regardless of what attributes they are blessed with. That's what I read in my devotional yesterday," Kendi stated.

Kendi looked down at her phone. She and Hope had just received a group text from Emma.

The text read: "Do you guys want to meet us at Mel's Diner? We're getting waffles with strawberries and whipped cream."

"Do you want to go?" Kendi asked Hope and Nola.

"How about if I drive you girls there? I have some potholders I made for the summer craft fair that I need to drop off to my friend Connie, and I can drop you off on the way because it is dark out."

"Okay," both girls responded.

◊ ◊◊◊ ◊

They jumped in the van so they could get some waffles. When they got there, Kendi wished she had cleaned up a little first, or at least bushed her hair and put on mascara. She was expecting a dark empty diner with Amie and Emma quietly eating waffles in the only occupied booth. Instead, the restaurant was loud, filled with teenagers, and was lit up like a Christmas tree.

Amie and Emma were in the middle of a large wrap-around booth surrounded by a bunch of Amie's friends from Chelan High. Emma was keeping everyone at her booth mesmerized with her animated stories and contagious laughter.

108

Since Amie and Emma's booth was super - crowded, Kendi and Hope looked for another place to sit.

Hope saw her new friend Sierra sitting with an attractive guy. Hope assumed he was probably her boyfriend Bryan, considering the way they were sitting. Across from them were two other boys who she guessed were possibly from the football team. In the far corner, Ben and Cody were sitting with some of their friends from school at a long table. Nearby, Kendi saw Hannah with her boyfriend Evan, his brother Drew, and Reed, Kendi's coworker from Brandon's. She wondered if Reed and Drew were dating. She would have to ask next time they worked together.

Basically, almost every kid between 15 and 18 in town was here in this diner tonight.

Kendi was a little uncomfortable in this crowd, and she imagined Hope was even more so. She thought she'd better take the lead and find them somewhere to sit. She looked around, not seeing an empty place.

Then, she heard a male voice yelling, "Hope! Kendi! Over here!"

The two girls turned toward the sound of the voice and saw Ryan beckoning them to come and sit with him and several friends at the long table.

109

Kendi and Hope hesitated because they could see that there were no empty seats, but Ryan waved for them to come back insistently. The girls gingerly weaved themselves through the crowd to where Ryan was standing.

"Kendi and Hope, this is Tanner and Tyson, have you already met?" Not waiting for a response, Ryan continued, "These gentlemen are going home now, so you can have a place to sit." Kendi and Hope started to protest, but Ryan said, "Relax! They have to be at school at 5 a.m. to lift weights with the team tomorrow, so they're heading out."

"I think I met you guys at the beach party at the beginning of summer," Kendi suggested.

"Oh yeah, I thought you looked familiar, Kendi," Tanner recalled.

"You're from Kirkland, right?" Tyson asked.

"Close…Redmond," Kendi responded.

"Well, we better bounce. Nice to see you, Hope and Kendi." Tyson addressed the girls, extending his hand with a grin. "Maybe we'll see you around town," he said as he shook their hands.

"He means *hopefully* we'll see you around town," Tanner said with a wink.

"Ignore him. He's a total flirt," Ryan admonished. "Just because he's tall, dark, handsome, and classy is no reason to pay attention.

110

Oh, but he's really cool, so you probably would be okay if you liked him."

Kendi smiled and sat down in the seat previously occupied by Tyson. Kendi was getting hungry but, by the time the waitress came to take their order, the kitchen had already finished serving waffles for the night. The girls each ordered a sandwich off the late-night menu and waited forever for their orders to arrive.

In the meantime, Ryan acted as host, introducing Hope and Kendi to whomever walked by. They were impressed that he knew most everybody.

Pretty soon, Ben noticed that the girls were there and he walked over to chat. "Are you girls recovered from the day on the lake?" he asked.

"Yes, we had a nap," the girls said in unison.

"Oh, my, you're even talking alike now," Ben shook his head. "Do you ladies work an early shift tomorrow?" he asked.

"I work at 8 a.m. tomorrow," Hope shared.

"I work at six in the morning," Kendi confirmed.

Ben looked at Kendi. "I'm not coming in tomorrow," he revealed. "Me and my parents are going into Wenatchee to look at some restaurant equipment. Some of our stuff is on its last legs. There's a big commercial bakery in Wenatchee that's closing, and they wanted to give us first dibs.

We're hoping to get a new proofer, and some other stuff. When we are there, we're going to get my senior pictures taken."

"Oh, cool! What are you going to wear for your pictures?" Kendi asked.

"You'll have to wait until I get my proofs," Ben smiled his gorgeous smile.

"Well, I'll hold down the fort at Brandons!" Kendi assured him.

Ben said, "I knew we could count on you!"

Hope and Kendi's sandwiches arrived, and they ate them hungrily. The crowd was starting to thin out, and the kids were consolidating at different tables, much to the chagrin of the waitresses who didn't know who ordered what.

Hope and Kendi finished their sandwiches and waited for their waitress so she wouldn't have to search for them. They paid their bills, then headed over to Amie's booth. "We're going to go home," Kendi told Amie and Emma.

"I'm ready, too," Amie said, climbing over two people to get out of the booth.

"Me, too," agreed Emma, who squished under the booth, dodged feet, and escaped.

All four girls got out the diner door.

"That was crazy!" Amie exclaimed. "Everybody showed up tonight! I wish Josh would have come.

He was in Seattle today doing orientation at UDub. But, still, it was really fun!"

"It's great that students have places to hang out so they don't get into trouble," Kendi told the others.

"Yeah. I know that we have students in Chelan who drink and do drugs, but we also have a lot of kids who just like to hang out," Amie stated. "Or, maybe I'm just naïve, and everyone's heading to a raging party after this," she laughed as they reached the porch of The Guesthouse.

"Looks like Aunty Nola's potholder drop off took longer than she expected," Hope noted.

"That's strange. Maybe she had something else to do?" Amie commented.

The girls didn't think much of it, but by the time they went to bed and she still wasn't home, they started to get concerned.

Hope texted Aunty Nola: *Just checking on you.*

A few minutes later, Hope got a return text: *"Sorry to worry you girls. We had a little excitement tonight, but nothing to worry about. I'll be home in about an hour. Don't wait up. I'll tell you about it tomorrow."*

"What do you think happened?" Hope asked the girls.

"Maybe car trouble or a flat tire," Kendi guessed.

"Maybe she stopped for gas and witnessed a hit and run!" Amie suggested dramatically.

"Maybe she has a secret boyfriend…" Emma contributed, and the girls laughed.

"That's not so crazy! Aunty Nola is pretty, and super nice. She'd be a great catch for some man!"

"Yeah, and apparently, she's an incredible skier as well," Amie added.

"I guess we'll find out tomorrow," Hope said firmly, hoping to end the conversation about a secret boyfriend for Aunty Nola. "I think I'll head for bed."

The other girls locked up and went up to bed.

Emma pulled out her devotional book and wrote a little bit in the lined portion after reading the scripture, then turned out her bedside lamp.

Kendi texted her mom about today's trip. Her mom didn't respond, but Kendi knew she probably wouldn't see the text until tomorrow. She settled into her cozy bed and turned out the light.

Amie and Hope fell right to sleep as soon as their heads hit the pillow.

CHAPTER ELEVEN

Coffee Shop Excitement

Kendi went into work at six o' clock the next morning and jumped right into getting hot and iced coffee drinks prepared for the morning rush.

Lynn was in the back making fresh pastries for the case, dancing around with music blasting into her headphones. Reed, the other girl who had been hired as summer help was already working on an order for four drinks that a local real estate broker had called in for his staff.

Ever since a somewhat disastrous day when they put Kendi in charge of baking, she was always on the schedule for the espresso counter. That worked out well for her because she was much more skilled at creating beautiful coffee drinks with foam decorations than baking attractive pastries.

115

She was getting to know the regular customers and how they liked their coffee. Since the coffee shop was right in the middle of town, many of her customers were vacationers, so they didn't stay long enough to start any real relationships. Sometimes, she got to serve the same customers on four or five of the days they were there, and she really liked it. She noticed that the tips tended to be better the more you got to know the customers–that was a little side benefit–but she mostly just liked to get to know people and where they were from.

This summer, she had met people from a variety of places. There were a few families who had come from as far as Europe and several who were escaping the summer heat of Arizona. The vast majority of Chelan's visitors were from the greater Seattle area. Well-to-do Seattleites loved coming to Chelan because it was close enough to come for just a weekend, but far enough from the craziness of the city that they could really relax and unwind.

Kendi loved trying to mentally guess where people were from before she asked them. Today, the people she met were all from Washington, except for one couple from California. One family was from Bellingham and there were a couple of local people on their way to work at the post office.

There was an older lady who had driven the ten-minute drive from Manson, and a group of young adults from Cashmere, a small town just outside Wenatchee.

Kendi was happy to see that Lynsie and Christopher, the couple she met the other day when she was at the lake, had stopped by for coffee. The tables in the shop were getting filled with people just relaxing and enjoying their day. She greeted them warmly and asked how Duke was doing.

"He's great," Lynsie reported. "We decided to leave him at home this morning because we didn't know exactly what we would be doing." Lynsie and Christopher sat down at the table to enjoy their coffee.

About an hour into Kendi's shift, the bells on the front door jingled, indicating someone new had arrived. Kendi looked up to greet the next customer and was pleased to find that it was Emma stopping by for an iced mocha on her way to work at Femley's. Kendi rang up her order, wrote something on the cup, and handed it to Reed to prepare.

Kendi asked, "Hey Emma, were you able to discover what happened with Aunty Nola last night?"

117

"Yes," Emma leaned in so she could talk conspiratorially in hushed tones. "She'd gone to Mrs. Riley's house to drop off the stuff for the craft fair, and nobody came to the door. She waited on the porch for a few minutes, thinking she was just in the bathroom. Mrs. Riley's car was in the carport, her lights were on, and it seemed like she was home. Aunty called her cell, but she didn't answer. She was beginning to wonder if something was wrong, so she headed around the back of the house to the backdoor and peeked through the window," Emma paused for added dramatic effect, then finally told her, "Mrs. Riley was unconscious on the floor of her kitchen!"

"Oh, no!" Kendi cried. "What did she do?"

"She called 911 and went through the back door because it was unlocked. She felt for a pulse and did CPR until help arrived."

"Did Mrs. Riley have a heart attack?"

"No! She was hit in the head by an intruder who stole her purse and some other valuables."

"Oh, no! Then what? Wait…hold that thought," Kendi put a finger up, indicating that this would just take a minute.

She helped a tall man who had just walked in. Out of recent habit, Kendi took a good look at him to try to get an indication of where he was from.

He looked pretty rough, like he might be a worker from a construction site. He was wearing dusty jeans and a faded blue t-shirt with no logos on it. He had work boots on that were pretty worn out. His blond hair was kind of bushy, like it needed to be cut about a month ago, and he had a green backpack slung behind him.

Kendi knew immediately that he was not a vacationer. She hadn't seen him around before, so she thought maybe he was new to town or working on some new construction here or down the highway in Manson or another small town.

Kendi pleasantly asked, "How can I help you, sir?"

"You can open up your till and give me all the money in it," he growled quietly but intensely enough for Kendi to know this was not a joke. He held out a canvas bag with a blue logo on it and thrust it in Kendi's direction. She fumbled around in a bit of a panic trying to open the register. Reed had heard what was going on, and she stopped making Emma's drink and stood still as a statue with her hands up and face drained of color. The man looked at Emma, still standing a few feet away. Her dark eyes were huge and she stood completely paralyzed. He hissed at her, "You—sit over there!"

119

Emma rushed over and took a seat at a nearby table as Kendi got the drawer open. She kept her eyes on the object in the guy's pocket that looked like it was probably a gun. One by one, the people sitting in the tables were figuring out that something was going on, alerted by Emma's hasty rush to sit at a table.

Kendi knew the cash drawer did not have much money because most people paid with debit and credit cards, but there was at least 70 dollars in the starting till, and she emptied out every cent into the dirty canvas bag.

The robber looked frantically around and noticed people trying to text or call 911. He yelled at the crowd to immediately throw their cell phones down on the ground and he drew his gun so they knew he meant it. He tossed his backpack at Emma and told her to put everyone's phones in his backpack. He yelled at everyone to get their wallets and purses out. Emma walked around taking the phones from the floor. He told her, "Forget about the phones, grab the wallets. NOW!"

Emma switched gears, properly motivated by the urgency in his voice and the weapon he was wildly brandishing, and quickly went from table to table collecting wallets and purses. Some of the ladies started screaming but were silenced by the man.

Kendi was trying to figure out how to get to her phone so she could call for help. She figured the best thing to do was to let the guy get everyone's wallets and leave. She was praying that no one would get hurt in the process. Kendi saw some girls approaching the coffee shop about to come in. Kendi caught one of their eyes and shook her head "NO!" with a grim look on her face. She didn't know if the girls could tell what was going on inside, but they quickly went back to their vehicle.

The robber turned to Kendi again and asked where the safe was.

"I don't know. I don't think we have one," she said in all honesty. "We don't take in a lot of cash. People use their credit cards to get the airline miles," she babbled on.

Geez, Kendi, shut up! she chastised herself silently in a moment of sanity. *He doesn't care about people's mileage cards.*

All Kendi could think about was getting the guy out of there. She could see that two of the men seated at the tables were trying to communicate something to each other. One was the man from California, and the other was Lynsie's husband. She was hoping they would just sit tight and let the robber get what he came for and leave before they tried to be heroes and jeopardized everyone's lives.

121

One of the men spoke up, "Let the ladies go and just keep the guys," he suggested.

"Shut! Up!" the man roared, pointing his weapon at the would-be hero.

Kendi saw movement from the side window and caught a glimmer of a dark shirt. From her observing of customers, she knew that nobody wore dark colors in Chelan unless they were wearing a suit or a police uniform.

Kendi was pretty sure that a police officer was sneaking past the side window so she tried to divert the robber's attention by calling, "Here, take the tip money!" The robber turned around to look at Kendi. At that moment, three things happened.

First, Kendi accidentally knocked the tip jar to the ground, loudly shattering the glass. Second, the two men rushed the robber when he was turned around to get the tip jar and wrestled the gun away from him. The struggle made the gun go off with a deafening bang that caused just about everybody to scream. Then, third, several policemen converged on the seating area coming from the front door and from the kitchen.

One officer took possession of the weapon from the California man and dropped it in an evidence bag. Two other officers snapped handcuffs on the perp and read him his rights, which he sneered at.

Another officer took the backpack full of phones and wallets from Emma.

An officer who was assessing the situation asked Kendi if Emma was with the robber since she had the backpack.

"No! She's my roommate!" Kendi blurted as several police officers escorted the robber out.

After the robber was safely out of the building some of the people wanted to retrieve their phones and purses and wallets from the backpack.

The police officer announced, "Folks, I am so sorry, but everything in the bag is evidence, so it will have to be photographed and catalogued. Unfortunately, you may not get your things back until at least tomorrow. Also, nobody can leave until we take all of your statements. Several officers are on their way to help so we can get through this quickly."

Kendi was grateful that her things had not been confiscated, nor had Reed's. She found out later that fortunately, Emma hadn't even thought about putting her own stuff in the collection bag because she was so busy getting everyone else's stuffed in the backpack under the robber's angry gaze. Kendi saw Emma discreetly send a text, and she was pretty sure she was letting Mr. Femley know that she was going to be late for work...really late.

Pretty soon, Lynn walked through the front door, as well as several more officers. Kendi had forgotten all about Lynn in the middle of all the chaos. Lynn came behind the counter to where Kendi and Reed still stood. Kendi started to fill her in on what happened.

"I'm so glad the tourists from the parking lot called the cops," Kendi said.

The officer looked up. "The call didn't come from tourists. It came from an employee."

"It was me," Lynn confirmed. "I had a tray of muffins, and I was coming through the flap door to fill the case when I saw that something was going on. I wasn't sure what it was, but I saw Reed with her hands up so I beat it out the back door, called the cops, and reported what I knew."

"Wow! Great job," Kendi said, wrapping her arms around Lynn's flour-dusted apron to give her a big hug. Emma and Reed joined in.

Then, the officers asked if they could interrupt and get the young ladies' statements. Each of them was paired with an officer to tell their story. Kendi had estimated that there was probably around $100 in the tip jar that was now scattered on the floor among the broken glass and definitely less than $100 cash in the till that she had added to the canvas bag, as per the criminal's demands.

The officers told Kendi and Reed to clear out since the shop would need to be closed for the rest of the day. Mr. Femley texted Emma and gave her the day off to recover.

Aunty Nola had heard what had happened and showed up to pick the girls up, even though The Guesthouse was just a couple blocks away.

◊ ◊◊◊ ◊

When they got home, they told Aunty Nola the whole story. Aunty Nola, in turn, shared her story about her friend Connie Riley who was assaulted last night. Mrs. Riley was now in the hospital recovering from the blow she took to her head.

Kendi asked what Mrs. Riley's burglar was wearing and, from that, it sounded like the same guy. They later found out that he had robbed a couple other houses in the middle of the night, but the occupants did not find out until they woke up.

The three of them prayed together, thanking God that no one was hurt during the morning robbery and praying for recovery for Mrs. Riley. They even prayed for the robber that he could learn about the saving love of Jesus and be reformed. The three of them cried from the stress of the morning and even laughed together as they discussed how funny it was when Kendi was explaining to the robber about people paying with airline credit cards.

125

It was past lunchtime by now, and Aunty Nola suggested that they go to Beaches for lunch after they called their parents. Both Kendi and Emma called their parents and downplayed the seriousness of the situation so their parents wouldn't be as worried.

Then, they got in the van and went to Beaches for a bite to eat. Amie and Josh had both heard about what had happened and had been praying nonstop for Kendi, but they didn't know Emma was involved. They sent their lunch orders to the kitchen and, since the lunch rush was over, they pulled up chairs and heard firsthand what happened.

Josh and Amie were appropriately freaked out, but proud of Kendi and Emma for their part in the story. They finished lunch, and Aunty Nola paid for the meal, tipping the wait staff generously, of course.

The girls had no agenda, so they suggested stopping by Joe's Jet Skis so they could tell Hope about the adventure.

Uncle Joe and Hope were not busy when the girls and Aunty Nola stopped by, so Kendi and Emma had time to relay the story. The staff at Joe's had heard that something went down, and Hope had tried to text Kendi, but she didn't see the text.

"Things like this just don't happen in Chelan," Uncle Joe marveled, "but this summer, we have had the car thieves that Hope called in, and now this robbery that Emma and Kendi witnessed, along with the break-in at the Riley house. Aunty Nola, you might need to start carrying a gun for protection," he suggested.

"I think I'll pass. I would probably end up shooting my foot on accident. I might be coordinated with water skis, but I know I would be a terrible shooter."

"Oh, yeah! Hope told me about your water skiing prowess. I might need to use you in my next commercial."

"I might be up for that," Aunty Nola countered.

"I'll have my people call your people," Joe laughed.

Kendi and Emma continued their world tour of Chelan with Aunty Nola driving them to Mr. Femley's General Store. The staff clustered around Emma and wanted every detail.

Mr. Femley took Nola aside and asked about Mrs. Riley. Nola told him that she had spoken with her an hour ago, and she seemed to be on the mend and would probably be discharged tomorrow.

"What a relief," Aunty Nola told the general store owner. "It could have been so much worse.

The Slaters' house was robbed, but they were out of town, thank heavens. The people who recently moved in on their street were home and asleep, but they didn't have much stuff because they had sold off a lot before they moved here."

"The thief wasn't the luckiest, Nola, even if he would have gotten out of town," said Mr. Femley. "He robbed the coffee shop that doesn't generate much cash, and he pretty much struck out on the houses he hit."

Emma and Kendi were ready to go back to The Guesthouse, but as they drove by the coffee shop, they saw the Brandons standing outside talking to the police.

"Please pull in, Aunty Nola," the girls begged.

The three of them got out and approached Ben and his parents.

Ben broke away from the group and gathered the two girls in his arms for a hug. "I am so glad you are both okay," he said, his voice low. Then, on a lighter note, he added, "Why do I always miss all the excitement?" The sudden shift caught the girls off-guard and made them laugh, which they were grateful for.

Mark and Rachel finished up with the officer, and then it was their turn to hug the girls and apologize that they had to go through the ordeal.

128

They wanted to hear all about it in the girls' own words, so once again, the story was told. Each time they told the story, it got a little smoother.

"I can't believe that Lynn was able to see what was happening and call the police...all because she was making the muffins," Mark said.

"Did they figure out where the bullet went?" Kendi asked.

"Yes. It ended up hitting the lower part of the wall on the side of the stage. It will be easily patched. I'm so glad it didn't hit a person. It sounds like we'll be able to be open again tomorrow. Kendi, did you need to take some time off, maybe get some counseling?"

"I think I'll be fine to work," said Kendi.

"Well, let us know if you have any signs of anxiety or stress. We will check with you during your shift to see if you need to take a break," Rachel said.

"I guess we'll need to get a new tip jar," Kendi admitted. "I kinda broke the other one."

"Well, we can manage that," Rachel assured her.

"How did your pictures go, Ben?" Kendi asked.

"We canceled them and busted on home when we heard about the break-in." Ben reported. "It makes more sense to get them done here in Chelan anyway."

"Well, we need to talk with the insurance company, so that is our next stop," Rachel said. "Thank you both for your cool heads. Without the two of you, the situation could have been much worse."

They went their separate ways after the girls assured the Brandons that they were perfectly fine.

CHAPTER TWELVE

A Special Meeting

Aunty Nola said she was going to visit Mrs. Riley in the hospital, and she would drop the girls off back home.

"Could I go with you?" Emma asked.

"Well, sure, darling, if you want to."

"I was thinking we could stop by the store and get her a teddy bear or something that she could bring home with her. I think she'll be afraid to go home since she lives alone," Emma continued.

"Maybe we can give her a card and write scriptures in it that she could look at if she is scared," Kendi suggested.

"Great ideas, girls." She turned the van around and stopped at Femley's. Emma chose an adorable teddy bear, and Kendi found the perfect card.

131

When the girls were selecting the card and teddy bear, Nola went into the grocery store and bought a bouquet of flowers.

When Aunty Nola got back to the van, and the girls were already inside, Kendi confessed that she didn't know how to find comforting scriptures. Aunty Nola had forgotten how new the girls were to Christianity, so she suggested they pull up their Bible apps on their phones and search for words like "fear" and "afraid" and see if any of the scriptures that popped up resonated with them. Both of the girls searched scriptures and decided on three each to write out in the card. They had intentionally chosen a card with room to write.

Kendi went first and wrote out her scriptures in beautiful brush lettering. Then Emma printed hers in neat little letters which turned out to be good, because the last scripture was really long.

Nola read what the girls wrote, and she was touched.

Kendi's scriptures were:

Psalm 56:3, Matthew 28:20b, and Isaiah 41:10.

Emma's scriptures were:

1 Peter 5:7, Deuteronomy 3:22, and Psalm 139:7-12

Emma looked at Aunty Nola and said, "It was good to finds these verses. I loved the last passage; I think I'm going to memorize it."

132

"Oh, Emma that is a lovely idea. Psalm 139 is a beautiful scripture. I learned it when I was young, but I think I would like to relearn it along with you. We can work together if you like. The whole chapter is long, but it will be worth the effort."

"I'll learn it, too," Kendi promised, reading over the chapter. "It would be nice to just know some scripture in case our phone battery needs charging, but we want to look up a verse."

Aunty Nola laughed inwardly at that comment because the girls were so tied to technology that they didn't even think about just using the Bible in book form as a backup to their digital Bible. That is one of the reasons why she loved hosting girls at The Guesthouse; they kept her informed on how the next generation thought.

Nola responded to Kendi's comment: "When we memorize scripture, the Bible says we are hiding it in our heart. There may be a day when the Bible is outlawed, and we will be glad that we have scripture hidden in our hearts where nobody can destroy it." She sighed. "Well, let's get over to the hospital. We need to leave before the shift change."

◊ ◊◊◊ ◊

Once they reached the hospital, the girls rode the elevator to the third floor and followed Nola down the hall to room 347.

There was an empty bed when they first walked in, and the bed closest to the window was where they found Mrs. Riley. She looked lovely and had the girls not known it, they would never have guessed that she had been knocked unconscious last night during a home invasion.

"How are you doing, Connie?" Aunty Nola asked her friend.

"Oh, I'm doing much better, thank you, Nola. And who are these beautiful young ladies?"

"This is Kendi Arnold and Emma Martinez. Kendi is from Redmond, and Emma is from Pasco," Nola replied.

"Nice to meet you," the girls chorused as they shook the hand she offered.

"Oh my goodness, I grew up in Pasco," Connie said

"Really? When was the last time you visited?" Emma asked.

"Oh, it has been close to twenty years," she calculated. "Yes, I went back for a wedding, but haven't been back since."

"It has changed a lot since then," Emma reported.

"Oh, yes, I heard that it has doubled in size and there is a huge new high school that is already bursting at the seams."

"Yes ma'am, the Tri-Cities area is huge now," Emma said proudly.

"Well, good. Maybe they finally have some good shopping. We used to have to drive all the way to Yakima to go to Nordstrom."

"Well, that store is gone, and we have to drive all the way to Spokane for Nordstrom now."

Mrs. Riley turned to Kendi. "And you are from Redmond…that means you have Bellevue Square nearby."

"Yes, my mom and I go there a lot," Kendi admitted.

"We brought you some stuff," Emma said timidly. She gave her the teddy bear that she had just bought at the store. The cuddly, light brown bear was dressed in a red pair of shorts and a white t-shirt with little red letters that spelled out "Teddy." She didn't know Mrs. Riley and didn't know if she would think it was juvenile, but somehow, Emma felt in her spirit that she HAD to bring Mrs. Riley a teddy bear.

Mrs. Riley took the teddy bear in her arms and cradled him. She actually had tears welling up in her eyes. "Oh, Emma, this is so sweet. After I woke up here last night I was confused and scared and the police told me what had happened. I prayed that God would help me to make sense of all this.

When I prayed, I told Him that I missed my husband so much. My husband has been gone for three years, you know. Well, then you hand me Teddy here. You probably didn't know that my husband's name was Ted, and I always called him Teddy."

"No, I didn't know that," Emma replied, her eyes burning with unshed tears now, too.

"God always gives us what we need, and I will cherish this little Teddy that my Pasco friend Emma gave me."

"We got you a card, too," Kendi added. "We wrote some scripture references that we thought you might like."

"Kendi, is this your writing? You write with such grace and elegance. You must be an artist."

"Actually, I kind of am," Kendi admitted. "I like to draw, paint, and play music."

"Oh, hopefully, I will get to hear some of your music this summer," Mrs. Riley suggested. "This is a good list of scriptures…just what I needed."

"We brought you flowers, too," Aunty Nola sat the vase on the shelf so Connie could see them."

"So beautiful," Connie murmured tiredly.

"Dinner time," the attendant announced cheerfully as she sat a plastic tray in front of Connie.

"Oh, thank you, dear, but I'm not really hungry," Connie commented sleepily.

"Well, I better get these girls home and feed them. They had a big day, too," Aunty Nola announced. She decided not to share the details of Connie's assailant's armed robbery of the coffee shop in case the news might further traumatize Connie.

Emma reached down and gave Connie a big hug. "It was so nice to meet you."

Kendi hugged her as well and gave her a kiss on the cheek.

Nola smiled, waved at her friend, and said, "Let me know when you are going to be released, and I will come and bring you home tomorrow. Love you!"

"Love you too, darling!" Connie said as they left.

"She was so sweet," Kendi commented as they rode the elevator down to the parking lot.

"I just love her," Emma stated, "and she loved Teddy! Now I know why I felt so strongly that she needed a teddy bear."

"It is so wonderful how you felt prompted, maybe by the Holy Spirit, to buy the bear, and you obeyed that feeling. God is so good," Aunty Nola said, smiling warmly.

◊ ◊◊◊ ◊

When they reached home, the other girls were already back, and Emma started to set the table.

"How would you girls feel about just getting pizza delivered tonight?" Aunty Nola asked her Guesthouse Girls.

"That sounds delicious," Amie said, and the other girls agreed.

"Amie, here is my credit card." Nola handed Amie the card. "Could you call in an order? I need to return a call."

"Sure," Amie said and ordered a couple large pizzas: one veggie and one ultimate supreme combo that included a little bit of every topping the pizza restaurant had on their list.

Hope and Amie had lots of questions for Emma and Kendi, and latter pair answered them all. Emma and Kendi shared about their experience at the hospital and how sweet Connie Riley was.

"It's terrible someone so nice had to be robbed and beaten," Hope stated angrily.

"I know, but she said that she forgave the guy who did it. She told us that was her first step toward healing," Kendi remarked.

"She is such a sweet lady, kind of like another Aunty Nola. Maybe we can have her come over and eat with us sometime. You will love her!" Emma gushed.

"She and Aunty Nola have been best friends for a long time," Amie mentioned.

The subject changed when the pizza arrived. Aunty Nola came down and everyone dug in.

The girls had wanted to play a board game together, so Amie and Emma looked through the game closet, choosing "Catan."

They spread the game out on the table and assigned colors. Kendi and Amie had played this game a lot with their parents, so they knew how to be really strategic. Emma had played enough to know the basics. Hope learned quickly and enjoyed the game. Aunty Nola was sitting nearby in the living room, doing her homework for the Bible Study class she attended weekly.

Then, the phone rang, and it was Mr. Femley.

The girls heard Aunty Nola's side of the conversation.

"Hello, George! Oh, no!" Nola said suddenly with panic in her voice

The girls stopped what they were doing and listened to the conversation.

"Uh huh…uh huh…I see. Yes, I'll definitely be praying. Yes, I'll text the girls from our Bible Study. Ok, keep me posted, please, George"

Once Aunty Nola hung up and returned to the living room, the girls asked her what was wrong.

"It's Connie Riley. After dinner, she fell asleep. Mr. Femley went to visit her after the shift change. He couldn't wake her, so the nurses came in, and none of them could wake her, either. She has slipped into a coma! I need to text the ladies in the Bible study to pray." She got busy typing a group text to the senior ladies' Bible study.

When it looked like she had finished texting, Amie came over and sat with her on the couch. The other girls clustered around her.

"Let's pray," Amie suggested.

"Okay, I'll start," Nola offered.

Aunty Nola gave a heartfelt prayer begging for the life of her friend. However, her tone changed as she continued, "Lord, maybe this is her time. I know that she is ready to be with You in Heaven if this is Your plan. Selfishly, we would like to keep her with us, because she brings so much love and joy to all of us. We are asking for Your will to be done, even if the outcome is different than what we would have chosen. You made Connie, and You love her. Father, Your will be done," Nola prayed.

Amie, Kendi, and Emma prayed, and Emma was weeping during her turn. Her tears came from the stress she experienced from her own encounter with the gunman earlier in the day combined with the connection she already felt with Connie Riley.

Her prayer begging for Connie's life was precious, pure, and earnest.

Hope was sitting there as Emma prayed, wondering what she would say when it was her turn. Emma went silent, and then, it was already Hope's turn to pray. She wanted to say something, but everything she wanted to say had already been said several times, much more eloquently than she could come up with.

Finally, she said, "God, please be with Mrs. Riley, and heal and protect her the best way You know how." Then, she added what she had heard before in church: "In Jesus' name, Amen."

"Amen," everyone chorused.

"Does she have children?" Amie asked after the prayer.

"Yes. She has a daughter back east who was planning to fly in on Sunday. George...I mean, Mr. Femley called her to tell her to come tonight if she could get a flight."

"Oh, that poor lady," Emma's tears flowed again. "She needs to see her mom before..."

"Emma, darling, I think you and Kendi better head for bed. It has been a very stressful day for you both, and I know you should call your parents and get some sleep."

The girls agreed and headed for bed.

Judy Ann Koglin

CHAPTER THIRTEEN

Parental Hugs

Kendi and Emma's parents both drove into town on Saturday morning, because both sets of parents were very upset about what their daughters had gone through, and they wanted to spend some time with them. Aunty Nola arranged for them to stay in one of her friends' houses.

Emma's parents left their younger daughter Riley with her grandparents because they didn't want her to know what Emma had experienced. They arrived in town and drove Emma to a quiet park on the outskirts of town so they could be alone with their daughter. Emma was still devastated, even though she tried to hold it back. When her dad grabbed her in a bear hug, she just lost it and wept inconsolably on his shoulder, her

143

little body shaking with her sobs. Her mom put her arms around the two of them, and the three of them cried together.

When they were able to get Emma calmed down, they asked her questions about her ordeal.

"Mama, I'm not really that upset about the coffee shop thing. I'm more upset about Mrs. Riley." Emma's parents listened carefully as she told them the story again about how she bought her a teddy bear and brought it to the hospital. She talked about how Connie Riley was from Pasco, "just like us." She talked about how she felt when she heard Nola on the phone. "It was so awful, Mom. We had just been with her, and she looked perfect, and she sounded perfect, and she even talked about shopping and Nordstrom and God."

"Oh *Mija*, we have been praying for you all the way here," her dad said. "We wanted God to comfort you."

Emma was taken aback. That was the first time she ever knew of her parents praying for her. This made her happy. She also hadn't heard them call her *Mija*, the Spanish word for daughter, for awhile! "Thanks, Papa," she replied softly. "I think I'm all cried out now."

"Would you like to go to lunch, Emma?"

"Yes, please…maybe the sandwich shop?"

"Of course, *Mija*," her mom said with a smile, and they headed to the sandwich shop so they could indulge in their legendary sandwiches on toasted sourdough bread.

◊ ◊◊◊ ◊

Kendi's parents had also come into town that morning. They had picked Kendi up and taken her to the elementary school playground, where they sat on the swings and had Kendi tell them everything.

Kendi articulated everything that happened in her organized way, telling them the scariest parts, like when the man waved the gun around; the funny part, when she started talking about credit card miles, and the crazy part, when she created the distraction but accidentally shattered the glass tip jar just as the men jumped on the robber and disarmed him. She talked about her relief when the police put handcuffs on him and took him to jail in Wenatchee.

She then told her parents the story of Mrs. Riley. While she wasn't as affected as Emma was, Kendi was still devastated to find that Mrs. Riley had slipped into a coma hours after their talk in her hospital room. Kendi's parents hugged her and told her how worried they were when they heard.

145

"Do you want to come home with us, honey?" her dad asked.

"You mean permanently? Like, quit my job?" Kendi shook her head vigorously. "No, definitely not!"

"I guess she likes it here," Kendi's mom said.

"I really do," she responded, thinking of the coffee shop, The Guesthouse, church, Slip and Slide, water skiing and her friends.

"So, you think you will be okay?" her dad pressed.

"Yes. Apparently the robber was a crazy guy, and he acted alone. He's locked up now. I feel perfectly safe."

"Okay…well, I hope this isn't tacky, but I am starving right now. Would it be cool if we got something to eat?" her dad asked.

"No, I'm hungry, too" Kendi assured him. "Can we go to Beaches?"

"Of course." Her mom's eyes twinkled. "You know I love that place."

"I had a sandwich there yesterday, but I really want one of their cobb salads today," Kendi shared.

"Beaches it is," her dad confirmed.

◊ ◊◊◊ ◊

Both families ate lunch and arrived back at The Guesthouse at about the same time. They sat down together in the spacious living room.

"I guess our daughters had quite a day yesterday," Mr. Martinez began.

"They sure did. I am really proud of both of them," Mr. Arnold stated.

"Kendi feels like she is okay and absolutely won't entertain the thought of coming home with us," Mrs. Arnold revealed.

"Emma, too. I think they love it here, despite yesterday's terrible experience."

"We do love it here!" both Emma and Kendi squealed, putting their arms around each other.

"Okay, well, I say we head home," Mr. Arnold said, looking at his wife. "I think they are fine."

Kendi's mom gave a nod. "Okay. Let me talk to Kendi outside first." Kendi and her parents walked outside together. "Kendi, you're sure you're okay if we head home now?"

"Yes. I appreciate you coming and talking everything through with me, but I'm fine. Go ahead and go home. You don't want to stay in Aunty Nola's friend's house anyway, that would be weird."

"True," her dad agreed. "Okay. Bye, honey! Call or text us anytime, and we will be there for you!"

"I know; you are the best!" Kendi gave them each one more hug and sent them on their way.

She went back into the house and Emma said, "I'm sending these two home as well."

"Yeah, it looks like you girls are going to be okay," her dad agreed.

Emma's mom seemed to hold the same sentiment. "I'm glad we came to see you and hug you, but it sounds like you are at peace now, right *Mija*?"

"Definitely," Emma replied. She walked them out, gave them big hugs, and sent them back to the Tri-Cities.

◊ ◊◊◊ ◊

Emma and Kendi decided to go get a coffee and see Ben.

He broke into a big grin when he saw the girls. "You two are a sight for sore eyes. You both look a lot perkier than yesterday," he added.

"Yeah, we both had visits from our parents. That was pretty cool," Emma said. "Oh, by the way, nice tip jar!"

"We'll have to watch this one," Ben replied, pointing to Kendi, "to make sure she doesn't smash it on the floor again," he winked.

Kendi grinned. "It was all part of my clever plan to distract the robber."

"Have you had many customers today, or were they scared off?" Emma asked Ben.

Ben gave them a shrug. "We've actually had way more people than usual because everyone is curious about what happened. That means more tips in our new tip jar to split at the end of the week, Miss Kendi!"

Kendi laughed. "Has anyone talked with Reed?" she asked.

"Yes. My mom has been in contact with her...she was shaken up like you guys, but she is doing fine. She'll be ready to work again Monday. She did say she wanted a raise, though," Ben joked.

"Okay, well, we actually came here for coffee, so could you get me a double shot caramel iced latte?" Kendi asked him.

"Of course! And you, Emma?"

"The usual. An iced mocha, please."

He busied himself making the drinks. Once they were complete, he gave them to the girls and said, "On the house. We'll see you tomorrow at church."

The girls nodded and waved goodbye to him.

"I can never figure out if I like him as a friend or *like*-like him," Emma chatted as they walked home.

Kendi nodded in response, but she was wondering the same thing herself. She did find herself thinking of him at weird times, though.

◊ ◊◊◊ ◊

When they got home that night, Aunty Nola filled them in on Mrs. Riley's condition. She had woken up from her coma, and they did some sort of brain scan. It looked like she was going to be okay, but they airlifted her to Seattle so the experts could carefully monitor her condition. Her daughter flew into SeaTac airport today, and she was just going to meet her mom at the hospital in Seattle, so it worked out perfectly.

That night, they had lots to thank God for, including Mrs. Riley's recovery, their parents' visits, and the love of friends.

CHAPTER FOURTEEN

Glamping Trip

Every July, the church that the Guesthouse Girls attended put together and hosted a mid-summer retreat for teens in Leavenworth. Their church was affiliated with a camp called Circle Q Ranch.

The Guesthouse Girls knew all about this retreat before they came for the summer because Aunty Nola was one of the chaperones, so this retreat was part of the lodging arrangement, and the girls had secured the days off prior to arrival.

Each of the girls was excited for the retreat. Amie had attended before, and she told the girls about the trail rides they could take on the camp's horses, the lake where they could kayak, the big forest to hike in, and the massive campfires around which they sang camp songs and roasted marshmallows.

The boys camped in rustic cabins, and the girls "glamped" in a climate-controlled bunk room in the lodge.

The retreat was only two nights long, but Amie packed like it was two weeks. She wanted to make sure she had perfect outfits. Hope packed the basics, and Kendi and Emma were in between.

Aunty Nola had to laugh as she overheard the conversations the girls were having as they packed.

"Do they MAKE you ride a horse?"

"Is camp food really bad?"

"Are there bathrooms in the lodge, or do you have to go outside in the dark?"

"Are the boys allowed to hang out with us?"

"What if you don't know how to kayak?"

"Can we shop in Leavenworth?"

And the all-important ones: "Is there a place to charge phones?" and "How is the signal there?"

The girls checked with their friends to see who was going to be there. The tally they came up with was that Ryan, Ben, Cody, Conner, Sierra, Maddie, and a bunch of others Amie knew were all planning to be there. None of the guys from the football team were coming because they were going to be at team camp that week in Wenatchee. The retreat officially started at four in the afternoon with an opening dinner for everyone in the lodge.

Since Aunty Nola was a chaperone and needed to be there by one o'clock, the girls got to arrive early, get first choice of the bunks, and settle in before the others.

Aunty Nola suggested that they leave Chelan at nine so they could be in Leavenworth when the shops opened. Then, they could explore the cute little town and have lunch there before they drove the six dusty miles out to Circle Q Ranch.

The girls were completely in favor of that plan and were up with all bags packed in the van by 8:45. Aunty Nola pushed play on a worship CD, and they sang along as they drove.

Kendi was sitting up front in the passenger seat, and Aunty Nola asked her, "Have you ever considered auditioning for The Voice?"

"Not really. Some girls from my school choir tried out when they did auditions in Seattle, but they didn't get past the producers. I think they were better than me, so I don't think I would have much of a chance," Kendi explained.

"Oh, honey, don't give up so easily. You have the voice of an angel! Maybe you should try out sometime? Every producer is going to have a different opinion. Pray about it and see if God opens the door for you, if that is what you want."

"Maybe I'll do that," Kendi considered.

153

Hope, Kendi, and Emma all went to large schools, so the topic changed from music to what it was like to go to a small school.

Amie gave some examples: "In a small school, most people have known each other their whole lives. Small towns don't usually have people moving in and out of them as much as in bigger places, so when a new student comes, it's more of a big deal. The new student can either be like a celebrity or have a hard time fitting into established friend groups. I suppose that could be the same anywhere."

Hope made a mental note of this.

"As far as teachers go," Amie continued, "sometimes, you get the same teacher multiple times. For example, I'll have the same teacher, Mr. May, for algebra two, geometry, trig, and calculus. That means I'll have just one math teacher for four years. My college prep courses usually have all the same students, so we are together in the same group of about 25 students for all of our core classes. We get mixed up in the electives, which is great, because I can finally see my other friends."

"What electives do you have?" Emma asked.

"Not many," Amie admitted. "When new students come, they are shocked to see we don't have as many choices as they are used to seeing.

154

We have choir, band, and some science electives, like marine biology. We have a drama class and an auto shop. I guess some people take PE as an elective in their junior or senior year. We only have one foreign language: Spanish. I know other schools offer French, German, and even Chinese, so we're limited in that way."

"What are the advantages of a small school?" Kendi asked.

"Well, there's only one high school in our town, so the whole town supports our sports teams. Most people know everyone else's names, even though they may not know them personally. Everybody may not like everyone else, but we're a community. Does that sound right, Aunty Nola?"

Aunty Nola gave her a nod. "Yes. I think you nailed it. The people in our town are supportive of the school sports because there aren't any cross-town rivalries to divide the fans. We are also supportive of all the students with all their competitions, school plays, et cetera. Many of us attended there ourselves, so we are tied to it."

"It sounds great," Hope couldn't help but say.

"It kind of is," Amie replied. "I just love this town and the school."

"You are the type of person who would be happy wherever you were," Emma commented.

155

"True," Amie said. "I'm annoyingly optimistic!"

The girls laughed at her self-characterization.

"Guess what, girls? We've arrived in Leavenworth!" Aunty Nola announced happily. "Have you all been here before?"

All the girls except Amie had been there only in the winter; Hope for a tournament, and Kendi and Emma for the town's tree-lighting ceremony.

"The summer in Leavenworth is beautiful, too!" Amie assured them.

The five of them went from shop to shop, enjoying the uniqueness of this little Bavarian town in the mountains. The architecture was beautiful, with the castle-like buildings that included balconies that over-looked the street. Some of the shopkeepers were even dressed in Bavarian costumes with full skirts and aprons for the women, and suspenders, shorts, knee socks, and hats for the men. The girls absorbed everything as they explored the town. They looked at decor in the year-round Christmas shops. They tried on crazy hats at the hat store and sampled delicious cheeses and chocolates at other shops. It was not crowded, and the five of them had a great time. Amie and Emma even bought a few souvenirs.

At lunch time, they went to a Bavarian-themed café and enjoyed yummy bratwursts and schnitzel.

The girls took group photos at every opportunity.

As they were walking through the sunny street back to the car, the girls saw a caricature artist. Emma asked Nola if they had time for a portrait.

Aunty Nola pulled out her phone, and once she checked the time, she said, "Probably not now, but let's plan to do that on the way out of town. I need to hustle to get to my orientation on time."

◊ ◊◊◊ ◊

They hurried to the van and took the short drive out to the ranch. They arrived at the expansive camp and drove by a huge stable with a bunch of horses grazing in the pasture. As they drove through the picturesque property, they observed deer walking nonchalantly nearby. The van pulled into a dirt parking lot in front of a mountain lodge. It looked exactly like Emma had pictured it to be.

As they grabbed their bags and walked towards the lodge, Kendi observed that the sky was a beautiful blue color with a few innocent-looking fluffy white clouds, and the mountain breeze was fresh and cool, a welcome relief from the heat that radiated off the hard dirt lot. She thought that she would love to paint the lodge someday. She knew her mom would, too, if she was there.

Aunty Nola led the way into the lodge and was greeted by camp staff who had arrived before her.

157

Paul, the director of the retreat, instructed them to quickly put their bags in the east room and then they could walk around and explore, but they couldn't be in the lodge during the counselor meeting. Aunty Nola and the girls climbed up the stairs to their sleeping quarters, which was a comfortable, large room filled with ten bunk beds for campers and two cots for the chaperones. Aunty Nola set her sleeping bag, pillow, and suitcase on a bed and went to her meeting.

"Wow…22 females, all in one room. That could get interesting," Hope murmured.

"We won't be in here much," Amie reassured her. They'll keep us busy most of the time."

The girls found bunks and checked out the bathroom near their room. It was equipped with a row of individual bathroom and shower stalls, plus a bank of six sinks and a long mirror, along with plenty of electrical outlets for hair dryers.

"Okay, this works," Emma sighed. "I was afraid we would have to go outside to find a bathroom!"

"Yes, it's rustic camping for the boys, but definitely glamping for the girls. We are so lucky to be in the lodge," Amie confirmed.

"Do the boys have showers?" Kendi inquired.

"Yes, but they're more like locker room showers in a bathhouse down a path from their cabins.

They say the water's always cold."

"It's good to be a girl," Hope commented.

"Let's go check out the ranch," Amie urged.

The four girls, led by Amie, happily exited through the back door by the kitchen and walked the quarter-mile path to arrive by the horses.

There were a couple people rubbing down the mares: one was a gray-haired man about 50, and the other was a rugged-looking teenager. Both were wearing dusty jeans, long-sleeved shirts, cowboy boots, and cowboy hats. The backs of their shirts were wet with sweat and their foreheads had drops of dusty perspiration clinging to them.

They look just like in the movies, Hope thought.

"Are you girls here for the retreat?" the older man asked, turning toward the group of girls.

"Yes, sir," Amie replied enthusiastically.

"Have you been here before?" the man asked.

"I have, but they haven't," she replied, motioning to her friends.

"You are in for a treat," the older man stated, looking at Hope, Kendi, and Emma. " The views from our trails are magnificent."

"Have any of you girls ridden horses in the past?" the teen boy asked.

Amie and Kendi both nodded, but Hope and Emma shook their heads "no."

The older man turned to his assistant and directed him to go and get the sign-up sheet.

While the boy was gone, the older man introduced himself: "I'm Dale, and my summer assistant is Justin. He came as a camper for several years when he was younger, and now, he has been working here the last few summers. Why don't you meet him in the stables over there and put your names on the list in one of the open time slots so you can get first dibs? After y'all have dinner, they'll post the sheets up--first come, first served."

"Awesome! Thank you, Dale!" the girls chorused and went in the direction of the stables.

As the girls were walking over, Justin was just coming out with a clipboard with the time slots.

Amie, always the planner, suggested that they sign up for the first available spots in case any of them loved it and wanted to do another ride later.

The girls each wrote their names on the sheet in the first slot which was tomorrow at ten o' clock in the morning. The sheet said that all riders must wear boots or heeled shoes.

"Oh, no! I totally don't have boots!" Emma cried.

"We actually have some loaner boots," Justin reassured her. "Someone who owns a western wear store donated some of her extras at the end of the season, so we have at least one pair per size."

"Oh, that is so great," Hope breathed a sigh of relief. "I don't have boots, and I wanted to try riding."

The girls introduced themselves to Justin and asked where he went to school.

"I just graduated from Connell High School, and I'm going to Washington State in August. How 'bout you?" he asked, directing his gaze at Emma.

"I go to Pasco High," she said excitedly. Turning to the other girls, she explained, "Pasco is less than an hour from Connell. We're practically neighbors. I'm only a junior but I'm going to go Wazzu when I graduate, too. Go Cougs!"

Justin grinned and replied, Go Cougs!" with a nod of agreement. "You girls should go check out the pool area. It was just expanded and it's great."

"Okay!" Amie agreed and led the way.

"Bye, Justin!" the girls called over their shoulders as they walked off.

"Bye..." he consulted the sign-up sheet, "Amie, Kendi, Hope, and Emma!" he called back to them. The girls took Justin's advice and checked out the pavilion area where the pool was. It had really expanded since Amie was here last year; it was still an ordinary rectangular pool, but it could accommodate more people than before. It was enclosed in a structure for year-round use.

The next stop on the tour was the pretty waterfront area which was home to a small lake. It was not big enough for water skiing, but it was definitely large enough to have a water trampoline and a swimming area. Amie told the girls that anyone could sign out kayaks and rowboats here.

The next stop was the archery range. Amie said that a lot of kids took archery lessons last year, but she didn't know about it until there was no space available, so she wanted to make sure to sign up for a lesson this year. Amie said that during activity time, they also have indoor activities that some kids take part in, like jewelry making, and they might even have an optional choir.

Once they were done with their self-guided tour, they arrived at the lodge parking lot and saw that a couple large church vans pulled up with the word "Othello" emblazoned on their sides.

"It looks like we might have another church joining us this year," Amie commented.

The doors of the vans opened, and about 25 teenagers spilled out, along with their sleeping bags, pillows, and duffle bags.

"Okay, let us go in first, and I'll let you know if they want you hooligans and all your stuff to come in yet," one of the bus drivers directed loudly to the Othello students.

Amie and the other girls walked up to some of the Othello girls and introduced themselves. They seemed like they were hot and tired from the long drive in the crowded van.

Another one of the drivers came out of the lodge and yelled, "Come on, girls, bring your stuff in! Boys, I'll drive you down to the cabins and give you your cabin assignment. All of you guys jump into this van...let's go!"

The boys crammed into his van with all their stuff and took off for the cabins past the stables.

While they were driving away, the vans from Chelan showed up. They had already dropped off the boys at their cabins and had come up to drop the girls at the lodge, a reverse of the other group.

When Kendi and the other girls walked into the lodge, they were greeted by a lady at a registration table. Each girl registered and was handed a schedule. The schedule showed that dinner was going to happen in about 45 minutes. The girls went up to their rooms and hung out with the other girls in their room.

At five, the bell sounded, and everyone came down for dinner. The girls found seats with the other girls from their room and ate a hearty dinner of cheeseburgers, baked beans, potato chips, corn on the cob, and watermelon for dessert.

After dinner, they played an intense game of capture the flag outdoors in the grassy field behind the lodge. After the game, everyone was really hot and headed over to the shade. The Guesthouse Girls migrated over to where Ben and Ryan and some of the other guys were standing.

"Hey, we signed up on the same trail ride as you girls," Ryan stated. "Looks like it'll be fun."

"Where did you see the sign-in sheet?" Amie asked.

"All the sign-up sheets are posted on the table by the front door," he explained.

"Oh, let's go," Amie raced to the back door of the lodge and darted across the main room to the sign-up table. Kendi and Hope were close behind, but Emma lingered to talk to the boys.

"What else did you sign up for?" Emma asked Ryan.

"Archery and row boating. We also signed up for the last timeslot in the pool."

"Okay!" Emma went over and joined her friends at the sign-up table. They saw the trail ride sheet that they had put their names on earlier. "I think I want to do archery," she commented to Kendi.

"We signed you up for that at eleven o' clock with us. We figured you would want to, and the slots were filling fast."

164

"What other options do we have?"

"I'm doing the choir practice at three, Amie is taking a diving class, and Hope is doing a hike up that mountain or hill, whatever it is," Kendi replied.

"Hmmm," Emma scanned the list of available activities. She saw that there was space on the pool sign-up list during the last session, so she signed up for that one.

Paul came up to the microphone and announced that this was the last call to sign up for the activity options, and they would be starting the group session in ten minutes.

There was a rush of people heading to the sign-up desk, so the girls went to find seats. Some of their friends joined them, as well as a couple of the girls from Othello who they had met earlier.

Joseph's band, which often played at Brandon's, had driven up after dinner, and they were going to provide the worship music for the retreat. Kendi was thrilled because she really enjoyed their music.

They led the group in four worship songs and turned the mic back to Pastor Paul, who spoke about loneliness and how kids can seem popular but really feel alone. He talked about how nobody is actually alone because Jesus is always with them, and they always have someone to talk with 24/7.

165

He passed little notebooks to everyone and had the kids take about five minutes to write down their reflections and answer a few questions in their notebook that would be useful for their small group breakouts. He then told them to look at the number written on the back of their notebook and go to the flag with that number that a counselor was holding up around the room. Each of the Guesthouse Girls had a different number and went to a different group. Aunty Nola was a group leader for a different group than any of the girls were in.

When they got to their groups, the counselor took the girls to different areas in the lodge, and some even went outside. Each group sat in a circle, discussed the talk Pastor Paul had given, and talked about times when they had felt alone.

Hope was in a group that included Hannah from Chelan and two girls from Othello. The other three girls went first and revealed things about their lives. One girl said she felt alone when she was bullied on the school bus and nobody tried to defend her. Another girl said she felt alone when she ran for student body treasurer, and she found out that she got hardly any votes. Hannah told how she felt alone when her friend moved, and she didn't have anyone to sit with in the lunch room.

166

This was a surprise because Hannah seemed really popular to Hope and she couldn't imagine her having trouble finding someone to sit with.

Hope silently reflected on what she would say when it was her turn. She didn't like being vulnerable and had constructed walls around her heart to avoid getting hurt, so talking to a bunch of strangers about such a personal subject was in direct opposition to what she wanted to do. In truth, Hope often felt alone because she was raised by a single mom and didn't have a dad or siblings. Her mom didn't have a lot of money like a lot of the other kids had, so they didn't get to travel, have expensive things, or live in a nice house. Even at The Guesthouse where she had three great friends, she felt different and alone, knowing that they each had families with two parents, houses, and lots of money.

Hope decided that she could just say something simple and not reveal too much of how she really felt. She wanted to tell the truth but not reveal too much about the depth of the loneliness that she often felt. She didn't want people in this group looking at her like she was an alien or feeling sorry for her because she was poor and didn't have a dad. She also didn't want them to spread information about her personal situation to others.

So, when it was her turn, she simply said, "I feel lonely sometimes because my mom works a lot, and I'm often home alone."

The group accepted that answer and moved on to the leader, who was one of the girls' counselors from the Othello group. She explained that everyone has times of loneliness, and there are a variety of ways to cope in those times…some ways are positive, and some ways are negative.

She asked the girls to share negative ways to cope with loneliness.

"Finding the wrong kinds of friends," one of the girls suggested.

"Definitely," the leader replied. "We can find ourselves hanging with people who are making bad choices since we think that we have no other options. This can lead to skipping classes, drinking, and worse," she mentioned. "What other negative ways do people find to deal with loneliness?"

"You already mentioned it, but drugs and alcohol," another girl commented.

"Yes. What else?"

"Dating the wrong guys?" another girl said.

"Yes. That's another big one. Loneliness often makes us question our self-worth and leads us to be impatient to fill the void, and we might be tempted to accept less than God's best for us.

Choosing the wrong guy can lead to more bad choices that can have lasting implications."

Hope thought of her mom, and her heart hurt. Hope didn't know what were the circumstances that led to her mom's teenage pregnancy, which resulted in her having a baby. Hope was just glad that her mom chose to keep her baby or else she would never have been born.

"What other negative ways do people do to deal with loneliness?"

"Building walls around you," Hope said flatly.

"Um…yes, that is a big one," the leader agreed, "Sometimes a person who seems rude is just a lonely person who fears rejection, so they choose to rebuff other people before the other person has a chance to reject them. In other cases, the lonely person is not rude or a bully, but they just close themselves off and are reluctant to make themselves vulnerable to others for fear of getting rejected. I've seen this many times with both teens and adults." She paused a moment. "This is a good time to ask the other question. What are some positive methods to combat loneliness?"

"Pray?" Hannah answered.

"Yes," the leader said with a nod. "Jesus says that He is always with us, and He will never leave us or forsake us." She looked at the next girl.

169

Talk to your parents about how you are feeling?" the girl responded.

"Yes, your parents are a great option. You should definitely try talking to them. They will have ideas to help you."

"Maybe talking to another adult?" the third girl suggested.

"Yes, you could talk to a youth leader at church or your school counselor. They might have some good suggestions as well."

Hope wasn't sure what to say because she herself was lonely a lot of the time. She thought of how she dealt with it and then said, "Maybe start a sport like running or join a team at school?"

"Yes, hobbies and sports are a good way to meet other friends and help combat your loneliness. But, in the end, there is an old saying that there is a God-sized hole in our heart that only He can fill. Until He fills that hole, we will not be complete. We can try to fill the void with other things, but they will not bring us true contentment."

Hope wrote that point in her notebook.

The leader went on, "When I was in middle school, I was a Christian, but I didn't fit in and I remember feeling so alone. I was surrounded by kids who were making bad choices, and I couldn't find any friends who were seeking after the Lord.

My prayer was that God would bring me a Christian girl to hang out with. He answered my prayer, and I met a sweet girl named Joy, a couple years younger than me who was a perfect friend for me. We wore the same size, and she had amazing clothes, so we traded outfits, helped out at Vacation Bible School together, and talked on the phone constantly. I practically lived at her house. When I was a little older, I asked God if He could give me another friend who was my own age. He answered my prayer and sent me another friend, Lisa, who moved into our town and went to my youth group. Never forget that God wants to give you the desires of your heart when they align with His will. Don't be afraid to talk to Him when you are lonely…or any other time, really."

Just then, Paul came around to all the groups to tell them to wrap up their discussions and pray.

Hope's leader and the girls prayed about loneliness and asked God to remind them that He was always there for them to talk to. One girl also asked that God help them to remember to seek help from their parents and others and make to good choices if they found themselves lonely. Another girl asked that God would help them to be sensitive to all the lonely people around them and to be a friend to those who may not have one.

171

Hope asked that she could remember to seek out healthy friendships. The leader closed them out, and the girls said "amen" and dispersed to their rooms to get ready for the night games.

It was dark, and Circle Q Ranch was in the mountains, so it was cold at night. The girls grabbed sweatshirts, applied mosquito repellant, and went out to the grass behind the lodge. They were each given glow sticks to carry around with them or wear around their necks.

They played a couple variations of tag, then formed a couple of large circles. Each circle of teens had three of their own glow-in-the-dark beach balls that they needed to keep in the air without actually catching them. The circle that had the last neon beach ball still in the air would be declared the winner.

Hope stood next to Conner, Sierra, and Maddie for this game. Her team dropped two of their balls. She was able to keep one of the beach balls still floating, but someone made a bad hit, and the final balloon almost dropped, but Conner made a heroic dive and wacked the balloon up a few feet. Hope ducked down and lobbed it up further and kept it in the air for another rally. In the meantime, the other team dropped their last ball, and Hope's team was declared the winner.

172

By the time the night games concluded, it was past midnight, so the girls went to their bunk rooms upstairs in the lodge, and the boys hiked down to their cabins.

◊ ◊◊◊ ◊

The next morning, the girls all took their turns in the shower and jockeyed for positions in front of the mirror. Emma and Amie sat up on Amie's bunk and put on their makeup using the mirror in Amie's deluxe makeup kit. Kendi was able to get a few minutes in front of the mirror in the bathroom, where she combed out her long, red hair and put on her mascara and some lip gloss. Hope took a shower and combed out her long, blonde hair and put it in a hair tie.

They met up with some of their other friends for breakfast, had a morning session with Pastor Paul, and then headed out for the activities that they had signed up for the night before.

The four Guesthouse Girls put on jeans, and Amie and Kendi brought cowboy boots along. They were joined on their walk by Cody, Ben, and Ryan. The seven of them talked about funny, and sometimes scary, experiences that they had with horses in the past. Emma became increasingly more apprehensive as she heard these stories.

173

When they arrived, Dale gave them the rules and instructions and helped everyone mount their horses.

Justin checked out boots to the people who needed them. Emma brightened when she saw him. He found the boots in her size and helped her mount the horse.

"I'm totally scared," Emma confided in Justin once she started to settle into the saddle.

"I picked out a super gentle horse for you," he assured her.

Dale assigned the placement of the horses based on the experience of the rider and the temperament of each horse. Justin's horse would go first on the ride, followed by Emma, then Ben, a boy from Othello, Kendi, Ryan, a girl from Othello, another boy from Othello, Hope, Amie, two more girls from Othello, and Cody. Dale would ride the last horse.

Dale had lined up the riders with experience between those who had ridden before. The riders lined up the horses and were given some final instructions. Once briefed, they took off up the hill. Every now and then, a horse would stop for various reasons, and once in a while, the trail would thin, and it would be a little scary as they had a steep drop off next to them.

Justin would check back every few minutes to make sure that the group was still together, and sometimes, he would stop the group so everyone could catch up. He used that time to talk to Emma. As apprehensive as she felt about the trail ride, being next to Justin put her mind at ease. Whenever she expressed nervousness, he would turn to give her a quick smile, and she felt better.

At one point, towards the end of the ride, Kendi's horse decided to go off on his own and ventured off the path. Kendi was not able to steer the horse back to the group. The horse, aware that he had a bit of freedom, began to gallop across the meadow as Kendi grew alarmed.

Dale quickly broke away from the group, chased down Kendi's horse, grabbed the reins, and steered him back to the line. He put Kendi's horse right in front of his for the rest of the ride. Kendi's heart was still pounding plus she was embarrassed. She felt like she was placed in time out because she failed to keep control of the horse. After the ride, Dale told her that horses occasionally get tempted by the fresh meadow grass, and go their own way. He assured her it can happen to anyone.

When the group reached the grazing area by the stables, the riders dismounted their horses with the help of Dale, Justin, and a couple other wranglers.

The girls pulled out their phones and took pictures of each other with their horses, with the wranglers, a big group photo, and just the Guesthouse Girls. Emma and Hope returned the borrowed boots to Dale and Justin, and soon, they were already off for their archery class.

◊ ◊◊◊ ◊

They had a time of group instruction in archery, and then each person got to try shooting a few arrows with their bows toward the target.

The target was colored gold in the center surrounded by a red ring, then blue, then black, and finally a white ring around the outside of the painted circle. The black dot in the middle of the gold circle was the bull's-eye, and the archer lucky enough to hit it received ten points. If an archer hit elsewhere outside the bullseye into the gold paint, they received nine points. Each color section also had two different point values, with less points awarded the farther away from the center of the circle that the arrow hit. The white ring on the outside of the target was worth only one point.

The best archer in the first round was a pretty girl from the Othello church named Angela. Ryan had met her at another camp that they had both attended and they followed each other on Insta.

176

They shot their arrows first, and performed well, and then spent the rest of the time chatting. Ben, Hope, and Amie also did a good job hitting the target. The others had some bad shots, but they also had some that made it onto the target.

In the end, Angela, Ben, Amie, and Cody had the most points, so they were called back to have a shoot off. Each got three arrows and a fresh target. Angela put one right on the bull's eye, one really close to the bull's eye, and the third one in the blue section for a total of 24 points. Ben had two really close shots, but no bull's eye. The third shot he made was in the outside ring. He received 20 points. Amie also earned 20 points. Cody's first shot was a bull's eye, and his second one landed in the gold, so he already had nineteen points, and it looked like he could be the winner. Unfortunately, his last shot missed the target entirely, and he ended up with only the nineteen points from the first two attempts. He resolved to check at lunch to see if there were slots open in one of the other sessions so he could redeem himself.

The top three were given plastic medals that they wore proudly. After a group photo at the range, everyone made their way up the hot, dusty trail to the lodge for lunch. Angela and Ryan stayed a bit behind the others, reconnecting.

◊ ◊◊◊ ◊

After lunch, everyone scattered to different activities. The last time slot of the day was at three o' clock. Emma had signed up for the pool that hour, as had Ryan, Ben, Cody, and several other teens from both churches, but mostly boys.

Emma had lots of fun playing in the water. They played keep-away with a spongy soaker ball, but, at only five feet and one inch, poor Emma didn't have a chance of getting the ball away from the guys who were a foot taller than her or more. Finally, Cody had mercy on Emma and released her from her spot in the middle of keep-away, and he took a turn.

Emma chose to get out of the pool and lie down in the sun to work on her tan. Her ears were full of water, and she'd had enough roughhousing.

Pretty soon, Ben came and joined her. They talked about their experiences in their other classes. Besides archery, Emma had done a baking session back in the kitchen and baked blueberry cake for tonight after dinner. Ben had been in a kayaking session. They stayed and talked until the lifeguard announced that the session was over, and they walked to their separate rooms for a shower and to get ready for dinner and evening activities.

Emma was glad that her naturally springy dark curls kept their shape when they were wet and didn't fall flat like a lot of the other girls' hair did. It saved her a lot of time.

Dinner was pretty good for camp food, and the girls all pronounced Emma's blueberry cake delicious.

The kids then got their notebooks out for the evening session with Pastor Paul. Tonight's topic was obedience. Paul told them that they would do the follow-up questions in their rooms or cabins tonight after all the activities.

After the session, the group did a night hike together up in the hills. It was a long hike, but because the weather was a lot cooler at night than during the day, it was manageable for most people. A few decided they couldn't go any further, and a counselor took them back.

At the conclusion of the night hike, they circled up by the campfire and roasted marshmallows for creative s'mores. Aunty Nola and some of the other counselors had set up a table with the usual graham crackers and chocolate squares, but they also added chocolate-covered mints for mint s'mores, chocolate peanut butter cups for peanut butter s'mores, and sections of a chocolate and caramel candy bar for chocolate caramel s'mores.

The idea was wildly popular with all the teens, and all the treats were eventually consumed.

The campfire was extinguished after the s'more festivities ended, and the teens were sent back to their bunks, where the counselors led them in a discussion about obedience to God and how that played out in their everyday lives. The girls were all pretty sleepy, but they tried to keep their eyes open and participate in the discussion before they drifted off.

◊ ◊◊◊ ◊

The next morning, there was time for a final swim or paddle in the lake. The four girls checked out a rowboat and rowed around the lake. Conner and Cody had a two-person kayak, as did Ben and Ryan. Sierra and Maddie took out a row boat with two of the girls from Othello.

They decided to hold an impromptu race, and each of the four boats lined up together. They were to go as fast as they could to a buoy about 100 yards away. It didn't seem that far initially. The girls switched off rowing duties every once in a while because it was exhausting.

The winners were Cody and Conner, followed by Ryan and Ben. Sierra and Maddie's boat was next, and The Guesthouse Girls brought up the rear.

"Oh, no! Now we have to row back!" Emma moaned.

"I'll get us started," Hope offered to a relieved Emma. Kendi and Amie each took a shift, and the ride back went smoothly.

Emma, Kendi, and Amie went on ahead to the lodge, and Hope walked with Maddie and Sierra.

Hope got back to her room, took a shower, and then joined the other Guesthouse Girls for lunch. She was quieter than usual as she rolled up her sleeping bag, packed her luggage, and brought her stuff to the trunk of Aunty Nola's car. They had lunch in the dining area, followed by another delicious chunk of the blueberry cake.

There was a final session with Pastor Paul before the retreat officially ended. He talked about encouragement and how much a simple smile, or comment could mean to another person. To illustrate his point, he had the kids spread out and find a person who they had done an activity with yesterday and give them an encouraging word.

Ryan told Hope that he was impressed with her archery, especially since it was her first time.

She said "thank you" and appreciated the compliment. She told Ryan that she was impressed how friendly he was and how effortlessly he could make conversation with people.

He said "thank you" and went on to give encouragement to someone else he saw who was standing by himself and looking lonely.

Hope got to thinking, and wondered if it was time for her to surrender her life to Christ. The truth was that she hadn't completely bought into this Christian thing yet, although she had only seen good things about it so far. She knew that true Christians like Aunty Nola, Pastor Paul, and Amie flooded joy and kindness to others. Hope didn't know if she could live up to that.

Her time of self-reflection was broken up by Conner. He had chosen Hope for an encouraging word, too, and he told her that he was impressed to see her help out Emma in the rowboat this morning.

"Hope," he continued, "I also wanted to say that you always show great character, and I really like you. I hope that we can spend more time together this summer before you have to go back to Lynnwood."

"I'd like that, too," Hope replied. Conner's comment lifted her spirits, and she felt a lot lighter.

Pastor Paul had them do one more exercise. He told them that in the first round, they mostly chose people they were friends with to give words of encouragement. Now, he was raising the bar a bit.

He had them stand in a circle and try to get in between people they never talked to before or didn't know well. He divided them out, two at a time, and asked them to give a sincere word of encouragement to someone they didn't know. He said it was harder to do that than to go up to a friend, and he wanted them to have some practice.

Hope was paired with a girl from Othello. The girl said to Hope, "I admire you because you are willing to try new things. I heard that guy saying that you did well at archery and had never done it before. I wanted to try archery, but I'm not good at most things, so I just signed up to swim every session because I am never willing to face my fears and try something new. I admire your bravery."

Hope just looked at her for a minute. Was she joking? She seemed sincere. *But,* Hope thought to herself, *I'm one of the most shy, intimidated people I know. How could she possibly believe that I'm courageous?* Hope reflected that maybe she was courageous about *things,* but definitely not *people.*

She then realized that she hadn't said a word in response to the girl's comment. Hope forced a smile and said, "I've always thought of myself as really shy and not at all courageous....but thank you so much for saying that." Hope knew that she needed to say something encouraging in return.

183

She had no idea what to say, so she looked the girl over carefully and told her, "I like how your pink shirt matches your pink hair thingy and your pink earrings. It's coordinated." She hoped she didn't sound stupid and defeat the purpose of the encouragement exercise.

She needn't have worried. The girl heard Hope's comment, and her smile lit up her face. "Oh, thank you for saying that! I try so hard to coordinate, and nobody ever says anything. I don't know if anyone ever notices me. By the way, my name's Kayli Olson."

"I'm Hope Stevens! Nice to meet you."

Pastor Paul went up the mic and thanked the group for participating in the encouragement exercise. He said it was time to go, that he would close the retreat out in prayer, and then get on the road. He prayed that the lessons learned this weekend would stay with them, and that each of them would recognize loneliness in themselves and in others, learn to forgive, and work on being an encourager.

After the prayer, girls who had formed friendships gave each other hugs before they went to their separate vans.

Kendi notice Ryan giving Angela a big hug before she entered one of the dusty Othello vans.

184

She tried not to let it bother her, but she thought to herself, *Hey, he's ours.* She had to laugh at herself because she wasn't from Chelan, so why was she getting territorial about Ryan? *I sound jealous! I better get over that,* she decided.

The counselors had to stay late for a short debrief meeting, so the girls asked Aunty Nola if she could pick them up by the horses when she was finished.

"Sure," she agreed, "but text me if you decide to go somewhere else."

"Okay," all the girls said as they hustled away.

They got to the pasture and saw Justin with a pitchfork pulling hay from a stack for the horses. They asked him if he only works, or if he gets to hang out and enjoy the camp sometimes.

"They don't let us fraternize with the campers."

"Will we get you in trouble?" Kendi worried.

"No. It's okay to talk to people who come up to us, but we can't join your activities, like your campfires, for example. There are plenty of times when I wish I could jump in the pool, but we have to wait for times when the guests aren't there."

"Oh, that makes for a boring summer," Amie commented sympathetically.

"Yeah. We have lots of adult staff members, but it is definitely not as fun as hanging out with kids in my own age group," Justin admitted to the girls.

185

"But during most of the summer, we have week-long camps, so we have actual staff counselors who are my age who bunk with the campers. We always do something fun after the last carload of kids leave."

"That's cool," Emma affirmed. "If you're bored and can get away, you should stop by Chelan."

"I might do that, Emma Rodriguez," he grinned.

Emma blushed, flattered that he remembered her whole name.

Just then, Aunty Nola's van pulled up, and the girls said goodbye and waved at Justin.

In the van, the good-natured teasing of Emma started and continued for a couple miles.

"Tease all you like, but I kinda liked Justin," Emma's curls bounced in emphasis.

"He seems really nice," Amie agreed.

"I don't know about you girls, but I want to stop by the Chocolatier in Leavenworth," Aunty Nola stated. The girls were in complete agreement. The five of them spent a delightful afternoon, but they decided not to do the caricature portrait after all.

CHAPTER FIFTEEN

Summer Night Jam

The rest of July passed quickly as the girls continued to work at their respective jobs.

Kendi grew closer to Ben as they worked together. They even had some jam sessions with his brother Joseph, mom Rachel, and dad Mark. Even Reed would join in on the fun. Kendi sometimes played the keyboards and sometimes she just sang. Occasionally, Ryan came by with his guitar as well, and Emma joined them when she was available. They tried out different songs in different genres like country, pop, rock, and inspirational. It was always a great time with lots of laughs and group bonding, and the Brandons decided that they would host an open mic session on the Saturday of Labor Day weekend.

Amie spent a lot of time at the resort. She had been training at the lunch counter the whole month of July, so she got to work with Josh a lot and decided that he was as nice as he was cute. Besides Josh, there were a few other summer staff members who she hung out with. Sometimes, the group of resort-working kids would go to the fire pit at the edge of the resort property and hang out around the fire. When they did that, Amie would shoot out a group text to the other guesthouse girls to see if they could join. On one such night, Hope, Emma, and Kendi were all able to make it, and they brought Ryan, Ben, and Reed with them. Ben had brought his guitar, and they sang songs while they enjoyed the breezes that blew off of the lake. It was another wonderful memory for the girls.

When the four of them walked back to the Guesthouse together after the hangout, Amie said, "Remember at the beginning of the summer we talked about dating when we were walking home one night?"

There was a chorus of "Yes, we remember," from the other three girls.

"I wonder how everyone is feeling about that now." Amie went on.

"Do you have someone you are interested in?" Emma asked playfully.

"I have to admit I have been thinking a lot about Josh lately. He hasn't asked me out or anything, so the question is probably moot. We might be heading in that direction, but who knows?" She shrugged. "However, I am changing training rotations tomorrow, so I will be working in the housekeeping department and probably won't see him much at all. I turned 16 in April, and Josh is almost 18, so I suppose we're old enough, but I think if he asks me out, I'll run it by you guys first and listen to your wise advice before making up my mind," she said with a laugh.

"Sounds like a good idea," Kendi nodded, thinking of her own dating possibilities. She was still unclear about whether Ben liked her, Emma, both of them, or neither of them in that way. She was also wondering about Ryan. She found it confusing and so weird that both of the two boys who she might like might also like Emma. She decided they should probably stick with their group musical sessions because no one should get hurt that way, and they all got to hang out together.

Hope couldn't even think about boys right now because in just a few short days, her Uncle Joe would be meeting with the current owners of the sporting goods store with his attorney Anne.

Assuming they were successful at hammering out the details, he would be purchasing the store, and Hope and her mom would get to live in Chelan permanently. She still had not told the other Guesthouse Girls about this possibility, but she was hoping she would be able to tell them sometime soon once the paperwork went through.

◊ ◊◊◊ ◊

The next evening, the group got together at the fire pit at the resort with even more friends. They arrived and left at different times but, at one point, the benches were full with Ben, Kendi, Ryan, Emma, Cody, Hope, Conner, Amie, Josh, Reed, Tanner, and Sarah, who also worked at the resort.

The sky was dark, but cloudless, so hundreds of stars could be seen in the night sky. The temperature was perfect; a warm summer evening with a slight breeze to keep it from being too hot. The tiki torches around one of the resort's pools a distance away provided a tropical ambiance.

Ben played his guitar, and the group sang and suggested new songs for Ben to play. They had some songs that sounded good and some that ended early with all of them laughing because no one really knew the words. After a while, Ben took a break from playing the guitar and Josh grabbed another log to put on the fire.

190

Amie gave a big sigh.

"What is that sigh for?" Ryan asked.

"I was just thinking that I love my life. Tonight could not be more perfect. This group is the best." Everyone nodded, realizing that a friend-group like this didn't come along every day. "But summer is ending in a month. Josh will go off to school, Emma, Kendi, and Hope will go back home, Conner will be doing sports, Reed will go back to Manson, and the rest of us will probably disperse into our regular groups. This time together is really special. I cherish it," Amie stated.

"I do too," Ben responded.

A chorus of "me too" also rang out among them.

"Speaking of dispersing, I need to head home," Tanner announced."

"I do, too. Early shift tomorrow," Reed offered.

"Me too," Sarah commiserated as she stood up and fished her keys out of her front pocket. The three of them walked to the parking lot together.

"Before anyone else leaves, we should do a giant selfie to mark the moment," Emma suggested.

"Too many people," Cody posited. "I'll just take a picture of you guys. I don't want photographic evidence of my bad haircut," he joked.

"Use my camera, it works well in dark lighting," Amie explained, handing her camera to Cody.

191

The teens squished together as everyone gathered around, and the camera picked up the light of the fire which illuminated the smiling faces in a perfect picture of a teenage summer night. Amie stole a glance at Kendi next to Ben, and fleetingly wished that Justin was here to be part of the group.

Cody handed the camera back to Amie, and she scrutinized the image. "Oh yes, definitely social media-worthy. I'll post it tonight and tag everybody. The group sat by the fire a little longer, making occasional small talk.

After the fire died down, the embers in the sunken fire pit were carefully extinguished by Josh and Cody, and hugs were exchanged, the girls practically floated home, they were so happy.

They sat down at the table, and Aunty Nola poured them each a fresh glass of lemonade.

Kendi said to the group, "Let's make a toast!"

"How about to more nights like tonight?" Emma suggested.

"Hear, hear!" Hope agreed.

And they raised their glasses as they basked in the delight of their midsummer adventures, as well as expectations of more summer nights to come.

<<<◇>>>

Books in
The Guesthouse Girls Series

Summer Entanglements

Midsummer Adventures

Late Summer Love

Upcoming Books in
The Autumn Collection

The Autumn of Kendi

The Autumn of Hope

The Autumn of Emma

The Autumn of Amie

These books can be pre-ordered, as they are released, through Maui Shores Publishing. Sign up for our newsletter for release dates, giveaways, and sneak peeks of what's to come.

www.mauishorespublishing.com.

About the Author

Judy Ann Koglin is a self-described "jill-of-some-trades, master of none." She grew up in the Seattle area, then attended Washington State University in Pullman, where she earned a degree in Business Administration and Marketing. There, she met Wade, and the two of them married and moved to Richland. Since then, she has enjoyed several mini-careers and eventually earned her MBA.

In her teens and twenties, Judy Ann enjoyed several trips to Chelan and found it to be a magical town. She also spent a teenage summer working in a charming beachside area on the Puget Sound, and she draws on both of these experiences to weave coming-of-age stories such as the ones in The Guesthouse Girls series.

In 2017 Judy Ann and Wade fulfilled a long-time dream and moved to the island of Maui. There, they enjoy spending time at the beach, taking long walks at night, and teaching Sunday school at Hope Chapel. Together, they are the proud parents of two boys, Tyler and Tim, and a daughter in-law Lauren.

Acknowledgements

At this point, Midsummer Adventures, the second book in The Guesthouse Girls series, has been written and published. I am grateful for all the people who loved the first book, Summer Entanglements, and have followed along to see what adventures Amie, Emma, Hope, and Kendi will embark on next. It is fun to sit down at my laptop each day and see what happens in the lives of these characters. It is generally as much a surprise to me as it is to my readers.

I extend grateful thanks to my faithful proofreaders and in-laws: Kay Koglin and Kathy Koglin, and my mom, Nola Schulenburg. I love their eagerness to follow the series and their careful attention to details that I often miss.

Once again, my insightful editor, Savannah Cottrell, was there for me, pointing out places that need more description and suggesting rephrasing to bring clarity to confusing passages.

Many thanks to my talented cover designer, Joanna Alonzo, for another great cover.

Also, thank you to Alex Stone who created my website and assists with social media.

I especially want to thank my husband Wade who is patient, wise and tech-savvy! Thank you for going on this book publishing journey with me and helping me through my issues, when the technical stuff seems too big a hill to climb.

Above all, I am thankful to God for this second book that He has allowed me to write and get out the door. He has given me many ideas for future books, and I am excited to see where He takes me on this journey.